Tears

of the

Heart

Gripping Tales of Love and Loss

BY

EVA TREMAINE & ALICIA J EVANS

"Writing Queenz of Queens"

Tears of the Heart, Gripping Tales of Love and Loss
© 2024 Eva Tremaine & Alicia J. Evans

Editing & Formatting: Carla M. Dean, U Can Mark My Word
Book Cover Design: Your Property Marketing Solutions

Paperback ISBN: 978-1-7359686-4-3
eBook ISBN: 978-1-7359686-5-0

Contact Info:
Eva Tremaine
Website: https://www.evatremaine.com
Email: Evatremaine@yahoo.com
Social Media: Facebook.com/evatremaine

Alicia J. Evans
Website: https://www.aliciajevans.com
Email: aliciajevans@myyahoo.com
Social Media: Facebook.com/authoraliciajevans

PRINTED IN THE UNITED STATES OF AMERICA

Dedication Page – Eva Tremaine

Spoken words fly away, but written words remain.

With every stroke of the pen, I am reminded of the profound gift of storytelling, a divine blessing that feels both sacred and precious. I am deeply thankful for the opportunity to share my words with you. Writing *Tears of the Heart* has been a journey marked by both joy and sorrow, a labor of love crafted to touch the hearts of those who have known loss. Some of these stories may be difficult, as the reality of death and grief can be overwhelming. My hope is that the tears spilling from these pages stir your emotions and allow you to connect with the characters and their journeys.

I dedicate this anthology to the loved ones I have lost along the way—cherished souls who have left their marks upon my heart and whose presence I carry with me every day. Though too many to name, they live on through these stories, honored and remembered with each page.

This book is also dedicated to you, dear reader, and

to the memories of those you hold close. May these stories serve as a mirror to your own experiences of love, loss, and healing, and may they inspire you to cherish and celebrate the lives of those who will forever reside in your heart.

To my devoted readers, who continue to support and uplift my work—you are the inspiration that encourages me to pour my heart into these pages. To my family, thank you for your unwavering love, support, and encouragement. You remind me to strive for greatness in everything I do and, if nothing else, to enjoy every moment along the way.

Thank you all. May these stories resonate with you and offer a gentle reminder of love's enduring power.

Eva

Dedication Page – Alicia J. Evans

There is something magical about spinning words to tell a tale

Tears of the Heart is dedicated to my family and friends who inspire me in all that they do. When deciding to collaborate with my writing partner, Eva Tremaine, on an anthology about love and loss, I had to go deep within myself to create stories that entertain and share a message. My inspiration comes from all who I have had the pleasure of crossing paths with. There is a strong, powerful connection between love and loss, and I pray that within these stories, it encapsulates the very essence of its power.

Lastly, I dedicate *Tears of the Heart* to you, the reader. You could have picked up any book, but you chose this one, and for that, I am eternally grateful. I pray that *Tears of the Heart* evokes different emotions within you that will keep you turning the page.

Enjoy the ride! Ciao!

Table of Contents

Tears
of the

Heart

Gripping Tales of Love and Loss

Shattered Trust

by Eva Tremaine

Once trust is broken, the damage is irreparable.

THE STERILE LIGHTS OF St. Barnabas Hospital flickered slightly, casting an eerie glow that exaggerated the long shadows in the bustling corridors. The rhythmic beeping of monitors and the soft murmur of voices filled the air, but no one paid much attention to the nurse walking quietly down the hall, a large duffle bag slung over her shoulder. To anyone else, she looked like just another staff member finishing her shift, tired and eager to head home after a long day. But beneath her composed exterior, her heart raced.

Her fingers tightened around the bag's straps as she neared the exit, each step feeling heavier than the last. The weight of what she was carrying, both literal and figurative, pressed down on her. The usual clamor of the hospital seemed to fade into an unnerving silence, amplifying the pounding in her chest. Every sound felt louder, every movement sharper.

As she approached the automatic doors, they hissed open, and the cool night air rushed to meet her. Her face was covered with a sterile mask to conceal her identity. She stepped outside without hesitation but couldn't resist a quick glance over her shoulder. Her face remained expressionless, a perfect mask of calm professionalism, but her eyes told a different story—panic simmered just beneath the surface.

The duffle bag shifted slightly in her grip, and a soft, muffled cry came from within. To her relief, no one noticed. She had patiently waited for the right moment and, within seconds, executed her carefully crafted plan.

Without missing a beat, she hurried to her car parked nearby, sliding into the driver's seat. The engine roared to life, and she sped away into the night, gripping the wheel tightly, her breath uneven. She had escaped unnoticed—at least, for now.

* * *

Cristina stepped back into the small hospital room, carefully balancing a tray of food in her hands. Despite informing the dietitian that she was a pescetarian, she had somehow ended up with chicken and rice for dinner. Exhausted and frustrated, she weighed her options. She hadn't eaten in hours, and her newborn son, Avery, was finally resting. Rather than wait another thirty minutes for them to fix their mistake, Cristina decided to head to the kitchen herself. After nearly fifteen minutes, she returned with a salad—not what she had hoped for, but it would have to do.

She decided to eat while waiting for her husband to arrive. He was stuck in traffic on his way from work and wouldn't be there for another hour. The discharge papers were already prepared, and a nurse had removed Avery's security monitor earlier, so she and her little angel were ready to go home as soon as he arrived.

Cristina thought about how Avery had been her constant joy since his birth two days ago, and she couldn't help but smile every time she glanced at him. Expecting to see him swaddled and sleeping peacefully in his bassinet, she turned toward it.

But something was wrong.

Her breath caught, and the smile vanished as her gaze fell on the empty bassinet. The room, once warm and familiar, suddenly felt cold and stifling. Her mind struggled to comprehend what she was seeing. *Where's Avery?*

Instinctively, her legs rushed her toward the bassinet before her mind could catch up, hoping that being closer would somehow reveal a mistake. But the bassinet was still empty.

The tray slipped from her hands, crashing to the floor, but the noise barely registered. A scream rose in her chest, but it remained lodged in her throat, trapping her in a slow-motion nightmare. Her vision blurred as panic flooded her body. Frantically, she spun around, scanning the room, her heart hammering in her chest.

"Nurse!" she finally screamed, her voice hoarse and trembling. "Where is my baby?"

Within seconds, the ward erupted into chaos. Nurses rushed in, drawn by her desperation. A senior nurse with graying hair stepped forward, her face etched with concern. She placed a gentle hand on Cristina's arm, but it did nothing to soothe her panic.

"Let's not panic," the nurse said, although her voice quivered slightly. "Sometimes babies are taken for routine tests without notifying the parents. It's possible that someone forgot to inform you. Let me check with the staff, okay?"

"No!" Cristina cried, her voice breaking. "We were already discharged! My baby didn't go for any tests. Where is he?"

At that, the nurse's expression shifted, and fear crept into her eyes despite her attempt to stay calm. She quickly instructed one of the other nurses to call in a Code Pink—a hospital-wide alert for a missing child.

"He still has his security monitor. We'll find him," the nurse reassured her.

But as the words left the nurse's lips, Cristina felt her heart plummet.

"No," she whispered, her voice barely audible. "His monitor was removed just before I left..."

The realization hit them all at once. Avery was missing, and the magnitude of the situation fully set in. The hospital went into lockdown as nurses and staff scoured the ward, checked records, and searched every corner of the building. Cristina sat frozen in her chair, numb, staring at the empty bassinet that now felt like a black hole in the room. Time seemed to freeze, but with each agonizing second, the weight of dread in her chest grew heavier and heavier.

Avery had vanished without a trace.

One by one, hospital staff came in with updates, but their words felt hollow. No one had answers. No one could find him. It was as if her son had disappeared into thin air.

As the sun began to set, casting long shadows across the sterile room, Cristina clutched the small blanket Avery had been swaddled in earlier—the last tangible piece of him she had left. Her husband sat at her side, also in complete shock that their son had been taken. Her mind spiraled, desperately searching for explanations that weren't there. She had only stepped out for a few minutes. How could this have happened?

Fourteen Years Later...

The morning light filtered gently through the kitchen window as Samantha poured herself a cup of coffee. Across the table, her fourteen-year-old son, Zaire, tapped away on his laptop.

"Mom, I've got this ancestry project for school," he said without looking up. "We're supposed to trace our family tree. Can you help me with it?"

Samantha froze, her hand gripping the coffee pot a little too tightly.

"Ancestry?" she repeated, her voice tense.

Zaire finally glanced up, catching the tension in her face.

"Yeah, you know, like where we come from. I need details about your side of the family and..." His voice trailed off as he hesitated.

He already knew he wouldn't get anything about his father. His mother had always told him that his dad left when he was born and that she had no information about him. Despite his many attempts to dig deeper over the years, he was always met with the same vague answers. Zaire decided not to push her anymore—at least, for the time being. He planned to use this school project as an opportunity to learn more about his dad, but for now, he would keep that to himself. It wasn't worth seeing his mother so anxious.

"You know, grandparents, great-grandparents. That sort of thing," Zaire continued, explaining the details of his school project.

Samantha forced a smile, though her voice wavered slightly.

"Of course, sweetie. We'll work on that. I'll find the information for you later."

Zaire raised an eyebrow, sensing the tension but deciding to let it go for now.

"Thanks, Mom," he said, returning his focus to his laptop.

Still, a strange feeling lingered. He always sensed something was missing. Where were his grandparents? His aunts, uncles, and cousins? His mother rarely talked about family, often steering the conversation away whenever he asked about it. He loved his mother—she had been everything to him—but as he grew older, the deep desire to know his relatives gnawed at him.

The questions about his family, particularly his dad, wouldn't go away. His mother's promise of helping him later never came, so Zaire decided he would start looking for answers on his own. He was extremely computer-savvy and vowed to use those skills to get to the bottom of this mystery.

For days, Zaire immersed himself in a sea of documents, websites, and every scrap of information he could dig up online. Each evening blurred into the next as he painstakingly pieced together a tangled and incomplete family tree. Names and dates taunted him, as if on the verge of connecting into something coherent. However, despite his efforts, a strange void lingered. The people he found seemed vaguely tied to his mother, yet something crucial was always missing. It was as though her entire past had been deliberately erased, leaving behind only shadows.

Late one night, with a half-eaten sandwich beside him and the quiet hum of his laptop filling the room, Zaire clicked through another round of local news archives. His frustration grew with each fruitless article—until he saw it. A headline that made his heart stop: *Infant Stolen from St. Barnabas Hospital – Still No Leads*

He sat there frozen, eyes glued to the screen, his pulse pounding in his ears. For a moment, he thought it had to be some kind of mistake, a figment of his exhausted imagination. However, the image accompanying the article told him otherwise. It was a photograph of a baby, barely a few days old. But it wasn't just any baby—it was him. Zaire stumbled into the living room and grabbed a childhood photo from the shelf. Holding it up next to the screen, the resemblance was undeniable. It *was* him.

His hand trembled as he leaned in closer, his eyes

fixated on the tiny crescent-shaped birthmark on the baby's arm—the same birthmark he had always known, one he had believed was unique to him. His breath quickened, and his heart raced even faster as he stared at the photo. There was no denying it.

He scrolled down the article, feeling his pulse hammering in his chest with every word. The story that unfolded was a nightmare. The baby in the picture had been Avery Matthews, stolen from the hospital. There were no clues or traces of who had taken him. Zaire's eyes flicked to the date: 2010. His birth year. His birthplace.

A cold realization swept over him. Samantha—the woman he had called "Mom" his entire life—was not his mother. She had taken him from his real family, stealing him away and severing him from the life he was supposed to have. He tried to convince himself that this could not be true. This could not be his story, yet there it was, right in front of him, staring back at him, daring him to face the truth.

He collapsed onto his bed, his mind spinning. A thousand questions swirled in his head, relentless and overwhelming. Who was the woman in the article, the one crying? Was she his real mother? Was she still alive? Had she ever stopped searching for him? And how had the woman he trusted most—the woman he loved with all his heart—built their life together on such a monstrous lie?

Zaire's world shattered in that instant. The woman he had adored, whom he thought could do no wrong, had now become the source of his deepest pain and betrayal. In the blink of an eye, he had lost everything—his trust, his past, and the love of his life. Now, beneath the wreckage, he had to confront the painful truth of who he really was.

* * *

The next morning, Zaire sat at the kitchen table with his fists clenched tightly and his heart racing as he struggled to contain the storm of emotions swirling inside him. He was waiting for his mother, but today felt different—everything felt different. He had to confront her face to face and read her expression for the truth. There had to be another explanation.

When Samantha entered the room, her usual warm smile vanished the moment she saw him.

"Zaire?" she asked cautiously, immediately sensing that something was off. "What's wrong, baby?"

Zaire stared at her, struggling to form the words.

"Is it Zaire or Avery? What's my real name, Mom?"

The question hit Samantha like a brick. She froze, her gaze fixed on him, silently praying her expression didn't betray her.

"Zaire...I don't know what you mean," she replied, but he wasn't convinced.

Without a word, he slid his laptop across the table. On the screen, an article about a stolen child glowed back at her. Samantha's face went pale. Her hands shook as she pulled out a chair and sank into it.

"Zaire...I can explain," she whispered, her voice trembling.

"Explain what?" His tone was sharp, cutting through the thick tension in the room. "That you're not my real mom? That you stole me from my family? That my whole life has been a lie?"

Tears filled Samantha's eyes. "I raised you. I love you. I never wanted this. I just...I couldn't bear the thought of losing you."

"You didn't lose me! I was never yours to lose!" Zaire's voice cracked as he stood, emotions bubbling to the surface. "Who am I? Where's my real mom? My dad? You stole me! How could you do that to them?"

"I am your mother, Zai—"

"No, you're not!" he shouted, tears now streaming down his face. "You're not my mother!"

Samantha's breath hitched. She reached out for him, but he stepped back, moving toward the door.

"I need to go," he said, his voice shaking with anger

and heartbreak. "Why did you do it? Why?"

Samantha looked away, silent.

"Answer me!" he screamed. "It's the least you can do!"

Samantha struggled for the words. "I couldn't have children. I wanted a baby so badly. I tried and miscarried three times."

"Why didn't you adopt? Why take me? Why me?"

"You were so beautiful," she said, her voice barely a whisper. "The most beautiful baby I'd ever seen. I was drawn to you instantly."

The weight of her words crushed him as he stood there staring back at her.

"So you decided to destroy my life? To leave my real mother devastated? Did you even think about how she would feel?"

"I did," Samantha replied softly.

"And you still did it. Without remorse." He shook his head, unable to bear another moment in the room.

"Zaire, please don't—"

"Don't call me Zaire," he whispered with his back to her. "I don't even know who you are."

And with that, he walked out the door.

Zaire left his home in a whirlwind of emotion, his mind reeling from the shocking revelation that the woman he had known as his mother for fourteen years had, in fact, stolen him at birth. His heart felt heavy with confusion and betrayal, unsure of how to process the truth or what his next steps would be. In a desperate search for comfort, he rushed to his best friend's house, where he poured out his heart to his friend's mother. As he recounted the story, the weight of the situation felt unbearable, leaving him lost and uncertain about his future.

* * *

Samantha had attempted to contact Zaire over the last forty-eight hours, but her efforts were fruitless. Zaire had texted her, notifying her that he was at his friend's house but did not want to talk. At least she knew he was safe. She anxiously awaited his next move, fearing the worst. Then the knock came, cutting through the eerie silence that had hung over the house.

Samantha opened the door to find two police officers standing on her porch, their faces grim and eyes set with a seriousness that made her stomach churn. Behind them stood Zaire, or rather Avery, as she now had to remind herself, and his friend's mother. Both looked solemn and distant. The air between them felt heavy with unspoken words and shattered trust.

"Are you Samantha Morgan?"

"Yes," Samantha barely whispered.

"Ma'am," said one of the officers, his voice firm but not unkind, "you're under arrest for the kidnapping of Avery Matthews."

The words, though expected, still landed like a punch to her gut.

Samantha didn't resist. There was no point in fighting what had been inevitable for so long. She didn't cry, didn't protest, didn't even flinch as they gently but decisively placed handcuffs around her wrists. As she stood there, bound by cold metal, she looked over at Zaire, but he wouldn't meet her gaze. His eyes were fixed on the ground, his shoulders stiff with emotions she could no longer comfort him through.

The door closed behind her as they led her out, the sound final and echoing in her ears like the toll of a bell. She felt the weight of everything she had done crashing down on her all at once. She had always known this day would come; she had spent years preparing for it, dreading it. But in her heart, she had desperately hoped it never would. Now, the reality was suffocating.

No matter what happened next—the court proceedings, the lawyers, the media storm that was sure to follow—it was all meaningless. The real punishment had already been dealt. She had lost the one thing that mattered to her the most in the world. She had lost her son. And nothing would ever bring him back to her.

Two days later, Zaire stood awkwardly in the living room of his birth mother's house. It felt strange being with someone who was supposed to be so important to him but who felt like a stranger. His birth mother, Cristina, hovered nearby, watching him with teary eyes.

"I never thought I'd see you again," she whispered.

Cristina stood alone, as she and her husband divorced after his disappearance. The loss of their child was too much to bear, and their marriage couldn't withstand the weight of such a great loss.

Zaire forced a smile, but it didn't reach his eyes.

"Yeah," he said softly. "It's...a lot."

"I know," she replied, stepping closer. "I don't expect you to feel anything right away. This is all new for both of us. But I'm here, whenever you're ready."

Zaire nodded, but his mind was elsewhere. He missed Samantha. Despite everything, she was still the woman who had raised him, who had been there for every scraped knee, every late-night homework session, every birthday. She had done something unforgivable, but it didn't erase the memories of the times they had shared.

"What do you want me to call you?" Cristina asked, trying to make her son feel as comfortable as possible.

He thought about the question and didn't have an immediate answer. He felt so lost in this new phase of his life.

"I guess Zaire for now since that's what my mom…" He paused. "…Samantha has been calling me for about fifteen years."

"Okay," Cristina replied, nodding. "Zaire it is."

* * *

Months passed as Samantha sat in a small, stark prison cell, staring at the ceiling. The days blurred together, but she didn't care. She had stopped counting the days after the trial. She had stopped hoping for anything.

Zaire had visited once. It had been awkward and painful. He hadn't called her mom, but she hadn't expected him to. She had stolen that right from herself.

Now, as she lay in the quiet of the prison, she realized it didn't matter whether or not she would ever be free again. She had already lost everything that mattered. She had lost her son.

The Fear of Losing You
by Alicia J. Evans

"PLEASE HOLD ON, KING! Don't let go! I got you!"
Mandala cried through clenched teeth.

Her grip was weakening. The sweat on her palms was causing her hold to slip.

With tears rolling down her cheeks, she pleaded, "Don't look down, baby. Keep your eyes on me. Please, Lord, give me strength."

With half of her body over the wall, Mandala's left arm firmly held onto the other side for support. Her right arm threatened to break under the strain as she held on to King. Closing her eyes, Mandala tried to summon strength from her ancestors. When she opened her eyes, she looked into her husband's gaze. Even in this moment, King's eyes radiated nothing but love for her.

"I love you, baby. It's okay. I'm too heavy for you. Let me go."

King said these words just as Mandala felt his fingers slip from her tight grasp.

Mandala shot straight up in bed. Her face and body were dripping with sweat, and her heart was beating so fast that it felt like it was about to jump out of her chest. Her silk bonnet was matted to her, and her hair was damp as if she had just stepped out of the shower. Mandala opened and closed her eyes a few times to adjust to the dark room. Holding her breath, she slowly reached across the California King bed to feel for her husband.

Mandala released the breath she had been holding as she felt King's warm body resting on the other side of the bed. Not entirely convinced, she inched closer so she could hear the whisper of his heavy breathing. Mandala let her right hand hover over his nose to feel his cool breath as he quietly exhaled after every inhale.

Finally confident that King was sleeping peacefully, Mandala left the bed to change out of her wet nightdress. While in the shower, her heartbeat slowed as she cried softly.

"I cannot keep having these dreams."

After her shower, Mandala abandoned the idea of getting any sleep and went into the den to watch a movie. She sat in King's oversized leather recliner with her knees pulled into her chest, thinking about her dream. Reaching over, she picked up one of the many framed photographs on the coffee table and admired her husband for the thousandth time.

Their wedding day was one of the best days of her life; the second was the day she actually met King. In their wedding picture, King towered over Mandala with his six-foot-seven-inch frame and two hundred and ninety pounds compared to her five-foot-two-inch frame and one hundred and sixty-five pounds. She wore a black two-piece jumpsuit with a black-and-white detachable skirt, while King donned a white tuxedo with a black notch lapel and a black vest. From the time she was a child, Mandala dreamed of wearing black on her wedding day, but everyone thought she was crazy. After their engagement party, Mandala shared her wishes with King, who was happy to oblige her. To him, it didn't matter what they wore as long as they were getting married.

Looking at the photo, Mandala felt a pinch in her heart. *Maybe getting married in black was not a good idea. Black is meant for funerals, not weddings.*

"What have I done?" she cried.

Mandala met King at the Dunkin' Donuts near the gym she owned. From that first moment, she knew he was different. He accidentally bumped into her as he was walking out, causing his iced latte to spill all over her. As he profusely apologized, Mandala found it hard to breathe. No, she wasn't hurt by the collision, but the mere presence of this man took her breath away.

He offered to pay her cleaning bill and buy her coffee or whatever she had been planning to order. When Mandala finally found her voice, all she could manage to say was, "It's okay." As she tried to turn around and leave, her craving for a hot pumpkin spice latte forgotten, the stranger introduced himself as King Mays.

What kind of name is King? Mandala thought, but when she looked up at him, she found the answer to her unasked question. With his deep brown complexion, wide eyes that bore into hers, large muscular frame, and commanding demeanor, he couldn't be called anything but.

King gave Mandala his cell phone number and encouraged her to call him once she got the bill from the cleaners. When Mandala never called, he camped out at the Dunkin' Donuts, hoping to see her again. After about two weeks, Mandala returned to the Dunkin' Donuts and couldn't believe King was there. He told her that he had been coming there every day waiting for her. Shocked and caught off guard by King's determination, Mandala agreed to give him her number.

And that is how it all began. King always made Mandala a priority. She didn't have to ask for anything; he was always doing for her. King showed Mandala how a woman should be treated, and Mandala loved him for it. Whenever Mandala was in King's presence, her heart burned with passion. King had a way of looking at Mandala as if she were the only person in the room. It didn't matter where they were; King's eyes would seek Mandala out and lock onto her.

As Mandala continued to gaze at her wedding picture, she brought it to her lips and kissed the image of her husband behind the glass of the frame. She loved her King and couldn't imagine her life without him.

Just then, Mandala heard the sound of King's heavy footsteps as he came down the stairs. She glanced at the wall clock and threw her head back in frustration. Not only had she not gotten any sleep, but she realized she had woken King when she heard him moving around.

"Another dream?" King asked, planting a soothing kiss on the top of Mandala's head.

He knew his wife was struggling, but he didn't know how to help her. Mandala had always been somewhat anxious when it came to him. She would often tell him that she didn't ever want to know what it would be like to live without him. Thinking she was being funny, he would just hold her and reassure her that he wasn't going anywhere. King loved Mandala and had no intention of ever leaving her.

Two years ago, he lost his baby brother Caleb at the age of thirty-three. Caleb's wife, Micala, had found him dead in their bed. It was unexpected. Micala had left Caleb sleeping in bed, but when she returned, he was unresponsive and cold to the touch. A month later, King began to notice a change with Mandala. She started calling him at work every thirty minutes just to say hello. She would insist that King call her each morning from the car on his drive to work. At first, he loved it and thought his wife loved him so much that she wanted to hear his voice. But he soon became worried that it was a little excessive. This morning, when he woke to her side of the bed empty, he knew she must have had another dream. Finding her in the den, sitting in his chair, his heart broke for her. How could he help his wife?

* * *

After finally ending the call with her husband, who made it safely to work, Mandala sat at her desk in the home office King specifically designed for her. She silently prayed that she would get some work done today. Being an entrepreneur had its benefits, which she didn't fully appreciate until after meeting King. He had promised her that she would never have to work another day in her life. As the owner of a fitness gym, Mandala was very independent and found it difficult to agree to give up her independence. However, she agreed to learn how to delegate. She now lets her managers and office assistants handle the day-to-day operations while she runs the business from home. This allowed her to be home for her husband every day.

What the last couple of months had shown Mandala was that being home all day gave her mind ample opportunity to roam. After her brother-in-law Caleb's unexpected passing two years ago, her fear of losing King grew to the point of being almost obsessive. She loved her husband, and when he was out of her sight, she worried that something terrible would befall him. Loving him was easy; losing him was something she could not bear. King had become her very reason for living. The way he loved her, no man had ever nor ever would. Mandala felt as though King's entire purpose for living was to love her, and the fear of losing him for any reason was crippling for Mandala.

Today, Mandala was determined to make the best of her day and get some work done while her husband was at the office. She felt proud of herself when she realized that half the morning had gone by without her calling King once. Meanwhile, King had texted her throughout the morning, keeping Mandala abreast of his day, and she loved him a little more each time for that. One of his many texts informed her that her lunch was being delivered via Uber Eats from her favorite salad bar.

Reading the message, her heart melted at how King always thought of her.

After devouring her delicious grilled chicken salad with crushed croutons and bacon bits, Mandala decided it was the perfect time to end her workday. Since King always did a quick clean of the bathroom every morning before he left, did the laundry on weekends, and had a cleaning service come once a week to tidy up their house, there wasn't much for her to do. So, Mandala settled on the sofa in the living room and flipped on the afternoon news.

A red banner with bold white letters reading *"Breaking News"* flashed across the screen. Mandala jumped up from the sofa and moved closer to the 57-inch television mounted on the wall. In record time, she reached for her phone, tapped on King's name, and immediately called her husband. When he didn't answer, she commanded the phone to redial. With tears streaming down her face, Mandala turned up the volume on the television so she could better hear what the reporter was saying.

"We have a ten-car pile-up on the I-78 express ramp. It seems a vehicle was attempting to access the expressway via the exit ramp. There are casualties, and no names are being released at this time. That is all we have for now. As you can see, traffic is backed up for miles. I recommend avoiding this area at all costs. As soon as we have more information, we will bring it to you."

The remote fell out of Mandala's hand with only a soft thump as it hit the carpeted floor. The room was engulfed in a cloud. She could no longer focus; she had to sit down. I-78 was the exact exit King would take to get home.

With her cell phone still clutched in her other hand, she tried to reach her husband again, but all she heard was his recorded greeting instructing her to leave a message. Mandala's head started spinning, and she began gasping for air as it had become difficult for her to breathe. The salty mix of tears and sweat rolled down her face, finding its way into her mouth. She attempted to swallow as her recently eaten lunch threatened to come up. Just then, she heard the slight click of the keyless entry front door disengaging. With all the force Mandala could muster, she took off running toward the door. When it opened and she saw King standing on the other side, Mandala leaped into his arms, wrapping her legs around his waist. With her arms around his neck, she squeezed him tightly while silently vowing never to let him go.

* * *

After a while, King managed to calm Mandala down and get her into bed so she could rest. But not before she explained how she had seen on the news that there was an accident, and she couldn't reach him. She told him how she immediately feared he was involved in the horrific scene. King explained that he had left work early to stop by Trader Joe's to pick up something to cook for dinner. While at the store, he realized he must have forgotten his phone at the office in his haste to leave. He had every intention of going back to his office to retrieve it, but traffic was horrendous, so he decided to just come home. After his explanation, Mandala started to feel a little better and agreed to lie down for a bit.

While his wife rested, King used her phone to call his office and ask if his assistant could drop off the phone when he left for the night. He knew Mandala wouldn't make it through tomorrow morning if he didn't have his phone so they could talk during his drive to work.

With dinner done, King went and checked on his wife. When he saw she was still sleeping, King let out a sigh of relief, happy that she was finally getting some rest. He felt awful for scaring her so badly. He made a mental note to always check that he had his phone before leaving the office. He usually did, but today, he was so excited to get home and cook dinner for his wife that it casually slipped his mind.

King decided to eat alone, not wanting to wake Mandala. After dinner, he poured himself a glass of Uncle Nearest 1856 Whiskey. As he sipped and savored the rich blend, he thought about his wife. King wondered if Mandala knew how much he loved her. His life was nothing until he literally bumped into her. She was the very reason his life had meaning, and sometimes, like her, he pondered what would happen to him if he lost her. With his drink finished and a plate for Mandala in the microwave, he cleaned the kitchen and headed upstairs to bed.

* * *

"King, please, hold on. I promise I got you," Mandala cried through clenched teeth as the pain of trying to pull King up was excruciating.

"King! King!" Mandala shouted. "I can't lose you. Please, baby, hold on."

In the dark of the night, King had fallen off the side of the boat. Mandala wasn't sure how it had happened. One minute he was talking to her about the fish he had just caught, and then he was gone. Her heart dropped, and she raced to the side of the boat. King knew how to swim, but could he manage in water this deep and cold? With the waves crashing against the side of the boat, Mandala's eyes scanned the dark waters for her King.

Finally, she spotted him and reached out to grab him. Why hadn't he put on the orange life vest? He had made sure hers was on and fastened tightly.

"King, please grab my hand. Please, King, grab my hand!" Mandala shouted into the night.

Feeling King's hand grab hold of hers, she tried to pull him out of the water. The vicious waves seemed to pose a bigger threat than she had imagined. Not willing to give up, Mandala pleaded with him to hold on. Just as she was about to dig in with everything she had, a wave surged, and just as quickly, she felt King's hands slip from her grip.

"Nooooo!" Mandala screamed.

Mandala's eyes snapped open, and she shot straight up, shaking and drenched in sweat as she tried to recognize where she was. As the dark bedroom came into focus, she slowly reached across the bed in search of her husband. Her fingers lightly rested on his forearm, checking to make sure his body hadn't gone cold overnight. She then tuned her ears to catch the faint sound of his breathing. It shouldn't be labored; a bit heavy with a low snore is what she listened for. Mandala finally released the breath she had been holding. His body was warm to the touch, and yes, he was snoring.

Mandala silently cried as she whispered in his ear, "I love you."

Mandala left their shared bedroom with a resolve she

had never felt before. She took a shower to warm her body from the freezing water in her dream. This time, she decided to put on clothes before heading downstairs. Sitting at the kitchen counter, she began writing a letter to her husband. When she finished, she slowly inhaled and savored the smell of cinnamon and vanilla wafting through their house. She then exhaled, releasing all that she had been holding onto. With determination, she walked out of the kitchen and into the garage, getting inside her 2024 Range Rover Evoque, a birthday gift from her King.

* * *

King rolled over and reached for his wife. Feeling the dampness of the sheets, he jumped up and called out for her.

"Mandala! Mandala!" he screamed as he rushed out of bed in search of her.

With a sinking feeling, King sensed that something was wrong—something was different this time. Rushing from room to room, he continued to call out for his wife. When he didn't find her in his favorite chair in the den, his knees buckled, and he dropped to the floor. In the midst of his despair, he heard a faint sound.

Picking himself up from the floor, he rushed toward

the direction of the sound. In the kitchen, he found the garage door slightly ajar. Suddenly realizing the faint sound was the hum of a running motor, he raced out the door, screaming his wife's name.

"Mandala! No! Mandala!" he screamed as he reached the running car and yanked the door open.

Slowly, his wife's limp body rolled out of the car and into his waiting arms. King wailed and screamed from the depths of his shattered soul.

"Why!" he cried into his wife's ear. "Didn't you know my life isn't worth living without you?"

King rested against the beautiful birthday gift that he had surprised his wife with. This was just one of the many things he had given Mandala in his quest to shower her with his love. He allowed his body to go numb as he rocked her and cried.

With his last breath, he whispered, "I love you, my dear Mandala."

* * *

Kevin, King's assistant, drove his car into King and Mandala's driveway. He knew it was late, but King would understand. Kevin was a workaholic, and staying at the office late into the night was nothing new for him. Not wanting to disturb them, he decided to leave the phone in the mailbox and send a text message to Mandala's phone to let them know where to find King's phone. As he exited the car, he heard what sounded like a man's screaming voice and rushed to the garage, calling out for King and Mandala. Not getting a response, Kevin frantically banged on the garage door while also dialing 911.

When the police arrived, they found King's and Mandala's lifeless bodies. A male officer handed Kevin a letter he had discovered on the kitchen table.

My Darling King,

I am sorry, my love. I can no longer live like this. I love you so much, but I live every day in fear of losing you. I could never go on without you. My life is nothing without you. I must leave you first so I will never have to know what it is like to live without you. Please forgive me, my love.

Yours faithfully and forever,
Your Mandala

The officer then shared that it seemed Mr. Mays found his wife's lifeless body, and his heart must have stopped.

"I guess what they say is true. You can die of a broken heart," the officer added.

Jeremiah's Prayer
by Eva Tremaine

Prayer is powerful. It can transform the most stubborn heart.
This story is dedicated to my forever angel, Angelique.

JEREMIAH LAY STILL IN a dark room, his back to the festive sounds drifting up from downstairs. The warmth of Christmas Eve was palpable everywhere except in his heart. He felt a familiar ache, the weight of loneliness pressing down on him as he struggled against the rising tide of emotion. The others were downstairs, caught up in the joyous activities that marked the season. Hot chocolate, laughter, and the scent of freshly baked cookies—all the ingredients of a perfect holiday celebration surrounded him, yet they might as well have been miles away. Jeremiah clenched his jaw, determined not to let his feelings show. He couldn't risk the mockery of the other children again; their taunts were still fresh in his mind, a wound that hadn't quite healed.

Tomorrow, Christmas Day, loomed like a dark cloud over his horizon. For Jeremiah, it wasn't a day of anticipation or excitement. Instead, it was a day when the contrast between his reality and the idealized version of Christmas became painfully clear. He would be reminded once again of what he lacked, the family he didn't have, and the loneliness that seemed to deepen with each passing year. So, he lay there in that small bed, willing the hours to pass quickly.

He turned his face toward the wall, hiding his tears from the world. Tomorrow would come whether he wanted it to or not, but for now, Jeremiah focused on the present moment, enduring the silence of his solitude amid the festive noise below. His temporary room was sparse, furnished with two twin beds, a small desk, and a dresser. Unfortunately, he shared it with Trevon, who seemed to take pleasure in making Jeremiah's life miserable. Since arriving at the foster home, Trevon had made it his mission to torment Jeremiah as if life hadn't already dealt him enough hardship.

The holidays can be incredibly challenging after such a profound loss, especially for a young child. For Jeremiah, it felt unbearable. Two years had passed since his mother died from cancer, leaving a deep void in his heart. The counselors at the JCCA Boys Foster Home assured him that things would get better with time, but the ache of losing his mother had not lessened. It took some time for them to adjust after Jeremiah's dad was killed in an armed robbery years ago; they never caught the man who pulled the trigger and turned their lives upside down. Yet, as mothers often do, Zuri managed to pull herself together and do her best for Jeremiah. Now an orphan, Jeremiah was still trying to adjust to his new life.

Jeremiah's memories of his mother paint a vivid picture in his mind of their close bond. Living in Harlem, they shared a modest two-bedroom apartment that his mother kept tidy, and there was always food on the table. Despite financial struggles, his mother's presence and love were what mattered most to Jeremiah. She wholeheartedly supported him in his passion for baseball, attending nearly every game and celebrating his thrilling first home run. This moment marked a high point in Jeremiah's life, as he felt a connection to his late father, imagining him smiling down from above.

One of their cherished traditions was cooking together for Thanksgiving. They would prepare a feast of their favorite dishes: turkey, mac and cheese, candied yams, homemade cornbread, apple pie served with Häagen-Dazs vanilla bean ice cream, and, of course, fried chicken. These meals symbolized not just sustenance but also the joy of sharing each other's company while pouring love into every dish. His mother made birthdays special, too, ensuring they celebrated with activities they both enjoyed—playing sports, watching movies, and indulging in favorite foods like chicken nuggets with French fries and ice cream for dessert from Applebee's. With his mother no longer physically with him, Jeremiah held these memories close to his heart. He deeply missed her, recalling her warmth and unwavering love that transcended any material limitations they faced. These memories served as a source of comfort.

He listened intently to make sure no one was nearby. Once he was certain, he slid out of bed and knelt on the floor, a habit instilled in him by his mother's teachings.

"Hello, God. It's me, Jeremiah...Jeremiah Morris. Mom used to tell me I didn't need to give my full name when I talk to you, but I want to make sure you don't mix me up with some other kid. Not that you don't know what you're doing, but I'm just making myself clear. I've been trying to do everything my mom and dad taught me, but I messed up a few times. Trevon had it coming, so I hope you forgive me. I know it seems like I'm always asking for something, but I'm really sad. I miss my parents so much, and I just want them back. I know I can't have them back, but I thought I would let you know.

"God, it's so sad and scary here. They turn off the lights at night, even though I asked them not to. Mom always made sure my nightlight was on in my room. But I guess they don't have fancy things like nightlights here. Well, the real reason I'm talking to you is to ask for a favor...again. I know you probably have a lot of kids asking for stuff, but mine is important. It's not stupid stuff like a new video game, so I hope you take my wish seriously. Can you please try to talk to my aunt so maybe she can change her mind and come get me? I tried to call her and wrote to her, but she didn't answer any of my letters. I even double-checked the address to make sure I didn't make a mistake. So, I was thinking maybe she would listen to you. Please, God, I really want to get out of here. Okay, God, thank you for listening. And please tell my mom and dad that I said hi and give them a big hug for me."

Jeremiah wiped his eyes and climbed back into bed, pulling the covers over his face. Although it wasn't bedtime yet, he had no reason to stay awake. He prayed for tomorrow to come and pass quickly.

Sandra, one of the counselors at JCCA, had noticed Jeremiah's absence from the festivities and gone to check on him. She stood outside his door, holding back tears. She hadn't expected to overhear his prayer, but the heartfelt plea moved her deeply and reignited her goal of finding Jeremiah a suitable home.

* * *

Sandra sat in her office, deeply absorbed in Jeremiah's file. As she read through the details, she couldn't help but feel a mix of empathy and frustration for the young boy's situation. Despite his generally cooperative demeanor, Jeremiah had faced significant challenges. The recent fight with Trevon appeared to be a clear case of bullying, something Sandra despised and actively sought to address.

Jeremiah's family history was equally troubled. With both of his parents deceased, efforts to place him with his father's relatives had largely been unsuccessful. His paternal grandmother was unable to care for him, and an attempt with an aunt ended disastrously due to her abusive relationship. Six months after Jeremiah arrived at JCCA, the agency connected him with an aunt on his father's side who was willing to take him in. Everything looked good on paper, and she even passed the initial assessment visits, which deemed her a suitable guardian. However, it later became evident that she was in an extremely abusive relationship, as her boyfriend frequently put his hands on her. On one occasion, while he was assaulting her, Jeremiah tried to intervene. The boyfriend turned his rage on Jeremiah, leaving him badly beaten with two broken ribs and a dislocated arm.

He spent months healing, both emotionally and physically, from that situation.

Attempts to find a suitable guardian continued, focusing on his maternal side of the family. The agency again ran into roadblocks, with only one aunt, Imani Chantal Morris, remaining as a potential option. However, that also led to a dead end. Sandra couldn't understand Imani's indifference toward Jeremiah. Living in California without any immediate family, Imani had shown no interest in taking her nephew in. Despite Sandra's persistent efforts to reach her, calls went unanswered and letters were disregarded. Even Jeremiah tried to contact Imani without success. Sandra vividly recalled the frustrating conversation she had managed to have with Imani months earlier. Calling from her personal cell phone in a last-ditch attempt, she was met with Imani's dismissive attitude. It was clear that Imani had no intention of involving herself in Jeremiah's life despite knowing the hardships he had endured after losing both parents.

"Hello. May I speak with Ms. Imani Morris?"

"Who's calling?"

"This is Mrs. Sandra Jacobs, calling from JCCA Boys Foster Home."

She could hear Imani suck her teeth, expressing her dislike at being called.

"Is this Ms. Imani Morris?"

"This is Chantal Morris," Chantal corrected her, as she didn't use the name Imani.

To her, Imani was a very ethnic name, and Chantal wanted no parts of it.

"Hello, Chantal. How are you today?"

"I'm fine. Can you tell me what this call is about?" she asked, wanting Sandra to get straight to it.

"I'll be quick," Sandra responded, noticing Chantel didn't even bother to ask about her nephew. "As you know, Jeremiah is here, and I wanted to discuss—"

"I already spoke with someone from the agency," Chantel said, cutting her off. "I'm a very busy person, and I really don't have time to raise a child." She paused for a moment and exhaled deeply before adding, "That's why I don't have any children of my own."

Sandra rolled her eyes and looked up at the ceiling, asking God to give her the right words to reach Chantal.

"Yes, I understand you're very busy, but we haven't been able to find a suitable home for Jeremiah, and I was hoping you would reconsider taking him."

"Nope. My answer is the same as before. I don't have time, and I wish you would stop calling my phone to harass me. It's not my responsibility or my problem."

Sandra could not believe how dismissive Chantal was being, but she persisted.

"Yes, I understand, but would you at least consider coming to visit?"

"I'll think about it. Look, I have to go," she said, hanging up the phone and leaving Sandra in shock.

That conversation took place over nine months ago. Sandra had been unable to reach Chantal, and Chantal made no attempts to contact Jeremiah. It was disappointing, and Sandra had all but given up on Chantal until she heard Jeremiah's prayer the other day. She would try again, but next time, using different tactics.

* * *

Chantal's morning routine operated like a well-oiled machine, even in the early hours. As she stood in her walk-in closet, the soft glow of the light illuminated her meticulously organized collection while she pondered her outfit for the day. Her wardrobe was not merely a collection of clothes; it was a reflection of her careful planning and refined taste. Today, she opted for a blue pinstriped skirt suit, a choice that exuded professionalism and confidence. The perfectly tailored suit accentuated her figure without sacrificing comfort. Pairing it with classic black pumps was a no-brainer, providing both style and practicality for the day ahead. Chantal's attention to detail didn't stop there. She reached for a mini Gucci purse, which added a touch of luxury to her ensemble. Though small, the purse was a statement piece, showcasing her appreciation for high-end fashion in every detail.

After choosing her outfit, Chantal proceeded with the rest of her morning routine, knowing that her appearance was not just about looking good but also about presenting herself in a manner that commanded respect and authority. As she readied herself for the unpredictable California traffic and the demands of her job, she did so with confidence, knowing that her choices for her outfit and accessories reflected her personality and professionalism.

She quickly showered and dried off, then began the careful application of various creams to brighten her skin and conceal any blemishes from head to toe. Chantal had been bleaching her skin for years, and most people who knew her before she started bleaching wouldn't even recognize her now.

Chantal carefully layered lotions and creams, concealing her true self beneath a veil of cosmetic perfection. Next, she meticulously airbrushed her legs, erasing every imperfection until they looked flawless. This detailed process required time, as each layer of makeup needed to dry before she could even think about getting dressed. Despite the tedium, Chantal was resolute;

she couldn't imagine stepping outside without projecting an image of absolute perfection. She scrutinized herself in the mirror for a moment, allowing herself a glance at her flat stomach before quickly averting her eyes. Time was pressing; she needed to dress quickly to avoid being late.

Chantal took one last look in the mirror, carefully checking every detail. Her eyebrows were perfectly arched, her makeup skillfully applied to create that flawless "beat face," and her eyelashes looked natural despite being false. Her bone-straight weave, made from the finest human hair, was immaculate and did not have a single strand out of place. Satisfied with her appearance from the neck up, she turned her attention to her body, which was an ideal size 8, enhanced by curves that seemed expertly sculpted, thanks to her highly paid trainer. After ensuring she looked impeccable from every angle, Chantal gave herself a confident thumbs-up and stepped out the door, ready to conquer whatever awaited her ahead.

Growing up, Zuri and Chantal were polar opposites. Zuri was undeniably her mother's child, sharing her light complexion and calm demeanor. In contrast, Chantal inherited her father's darker skin, which made her resent not only Zuri but also their mother for somehow passing the "good" genes to Zuri. This resentment led Chantal to distance herself from the family. Zuri often questioned her mother about whether Chantal was truly her blood sister. They never had a sisterly bond, and as Zuri grew older, she came to accept that Chantal was—and always would be—selfish and vain. Zuri made efforts to cultivate a relationship with Chantal, often taking the initiative to reach out and establish some form of sisterly connection, but she was unsuccessful. As adults, they rarely spoke on the phone, and Chantal almost didn't make it to their mother's funeral. She was always booked and busy, leaving no time for her family. She had a lukewarm relationship with Jeremiah, which was manageable until now. But now, he needed her more than ever because he was truly alone.

On the surface, Chantal displayed a facade of composure, yet internally, she grappled with deep insecurities and a strong need for approval from her Caucasian peers, sometimes distancing herself from her own community. From a young age, Chantal's discomfort with her identity was evident to her mother, who tirelessly highlighted the beauty inherent in her daughters. Despite her mother's efforts, Chantal found it difficult to embrace these affirmations, perpetuating her internal struggle with self-acceptance.

When Chantal was eight years old, a traumatic event deeply impacted her view of herself and those around her. Bullied by classmates, who were also African American but had lighter skin, she faced relentless torment in the school bathroom. They cruelly mocked her dark skin, comparing it to feces in the toilet, which left Chantal heartbroken and in tears. Although she kept this painful experience to herself, it ignited a deep-seated self-loathing and a desire to distance herself from her identity. This incident marked the beginning of her transformation from Imani to Chantal—a journey characterized by a fixation on her outward appearance and a lack of empathy.

* * *

Jeremiah was passionate about sci-fi anime and spent many hours sketching striking African American characters. In the arts and crafts room, he carefully designed a new female anime character, quietly naming her "Mom." A well-worn comic book served as his muse, inspiring him to create the perfect image. Over the years, Jeremiah's artistic abilities had flourished, and he now wielded his drawing tools with confidence and ease.

Peering into the room, Sandra spotted Jeremiah and another child sitting quietly. She lingered at the door, observing the peaceful scene Jeremiah seemed to embody.

"Jeremiah, can I talk to you for a moment?" she called out.

Jeremiah gathered his things and walked with Sandra to her office.

"How are you doing today?" Sandra asked gently.

"I'm fine," Jeremiah replied softly.

Since arriving at JCCA, he hadn't been very talkative.

"I noticed you were drawing. Can I see?" Sandra inquired.

Jeremiah took his drawing out of his bag, studying it for a moment before passing it to Sandra.

"Wow, this is amazing," Sandra exclaimed, admiring the intricate and detailed artwork. "What do you call this one?"

"I haven't given her a name yet," Jeremiah replied.

"She's beautiful," Sandra praised.

"Thanks," Jeremiah said as he gently tucked the drawing back into his sketchbook.

"I have some good news for you," Sandra went on.

Jeremiah's eyes lit up with hope.

"We're changing your room. You'll be rooming with Charles. Would you like that?"

Trying to hide his disappointment, Jeremiah looked down. While he was glad to be away from Trevon, he had hoped to receive news that his aunt would be coming for him.

Sandra noticed his reaction but wanted to offer him something positive.

"And guess what?" she added with a wink. "There will be a nightlight in the room."

Jeremiah smiled gratefully, appreciating the small gesture.

"Thank you. May I go now?" he asked.

"Sure," Sandra replied, nodding.

As Jeremiah left the office, Sandra resolved to find him a suitable home. She saw his longing for happiness and prayed she could bring some joy into his life, especially after he had endured so much disappointment.

* * *

Chantal settled into her seat, pleased that her company had upgraded her and the team to business class for their seven-hour flight to New York. With an important client meeting ahead, where she would lead the presentation for a lucrative marketing campaign, comfort was essential. As the crew had yet to announce for passengers to put their electronic devices on airplane mode, she took the opportunity to finalize her slides, confident that her last-minute tweaks would secure the deal. Once she closed her laptop, she prepared for takeoff. Known for her social media prowess, she couldn't resist snapping a quick selfie and posting it on Facebook with the caption: *Off to New York! Wish me luck!* Being careful to keep the message vague enough to maintain client confidentiality, she ensured it wouldn't jeopardize the deal. Relaxing into her seat, she began rehearsing her pitch, knowing that making a stellar first impression was crucial.

"You've got this," she whispered to herself, boosting her confidence for the upcoming presentation.

While Chantal meticulously maintained a façade of perfection at work, Sandra quietly plotted her strategy to connect with her, hoping to unite her with Jeremiah. Her latest tactic involved following Chantal on social media using a pseudonym. Sandra created a persona with a captivating bio designed to piqué Chantal's interest, successfully attracting her attention. However, Sandra still needed to find an opportunity to draw Chantal closer. Everything changed when Sandra came across Chantal's recent post announcing her trip to New York. Recognizing this as a pivotal moment, Sandra knew she had to act swiftly before losing her chance.

Chantal had arranged a week-long stay in New York, complete with a carefully structured itinerary. The first two days focused on strategy sessions with her team, followed by a lavish dinner entertaining a potential client at one of New York's finest restaurants. The next two days were devoted to intensive presentations aimed at securing the new client, with hopes that the final day would culminate in a celebratory success.

Chantal's presentation on the first day was a triumph, impressing senior leadership with a compelling rationale, a detailed implementation strategy that provided adaptable options, and a contingency plan for varying levels of client engagement. Presenting with confidence before both the client and her team, Chantal exuded poise, expertise, and deep knowledge of the subject matter. The deal was nearly finalized, with Daniel from Accounting crunching the numbers to ensure alignment with the budget. Daniel's impressive delivery also captivated the audience, leaving the entire team elated and highly confident in their imminent success.

Chantal couldn't stop smiling as her team congratulated her on a job well done. It was two o'clock in the afternoon, and they anticipated hearing by noon the following day whether their proposal had been approved. If all went as planned, they would enjoy a celebratory outing the next day before heading back to California. Chantal knew she did her thing, and her boss was very impressed. She was already earning a salary of two hundred and fifteen thousand dollars per year, but if they landed this client, she could be making close to three hundred thousand by the end of the year.

Her phone rang, and she answered it, not recognizing the number. Chantal often received calls from referrals and various networking events, so she didn't ignore unknown numbers.

"Hello, Chantal Morris. How can I assist you today?"

"Hello, Chantal. This is Sandra, the social worker from JCCA Boys Home. How are you doing?"

"I'm well," Chantal replied, determined not to let anything ruin her mood.

"Last time we spoke, you mentioned you might consider visiting Jeremiah. Have you had a chance to think about it?"

Glancing at her watch and realizing she had the rest of the day off, Chantal asked, "Where are you located?"

Sandra quickly recited the address, hoping this time Chantal would agree to visit Jeremiah.

Knowing New York City well, Chantal estimated it wouldn't take her more than forty-five minutes to reach JCCA.

"I'm actually in New York on business right now, so I could stop by before heading back to California."

"Oh, really?" Sandra exclaimed, pretending she didn't already know. "I'm sure Jeremiah would love to see you."

"What time does visitation end?"

"You can visit as late as you like," Sandra assured her, ready to seek approval for any necessary exceptions.

"Okay, I'll be there in about an hour."

"Thanks so much, Chantal. When you arrive, just ask for me. We're looking forward to seeing you."

"Alright, bye," Chantal said, ending the call and briefly questioning her decision.

After hanging up, Sandra thanked God for His grace. She prayed earnestly that Chantal would keep her word, but Sandra decided not to tell Jeremiah until she saw Chantal in the flesh to avoid the possibility of him being disappointed if she didn't.

* * *

Chantal arrived at JCCA in just under forty minutes, as she had estimated during her Uber ride. During the ride, she pondered what she would say to Jeremiah. Having spent little time with him before, she felt unsure about how to connect with a pre-teen boy. If it had been a girl, she might have felt more at ease, but what commonalities did they share aside from being related?

As she wrestled with her thoughts, Chantal briefly considered telling the driver to turn around. However, Sandra's words echoed in her mind—*Jeremiah had no one.* Despite her hesitations, Chantal couldn't ignore the compassion she felt for her nephew, who had lost both his parents. Although she and Zuri hadn't been particularly close, Chantal couldn't deny that she missed her sister at times. Still, deep down, she harbored resentment towards Zuri. She couldn't bear children herself, so Jeremiah's birth only intensified these feelings. It seemed unfair to her that Zuri, who already had so much, could become a mother effortlessly. Despite these conflicted emotions, Chantal knew Jeremiah needed someone to step in and help him. She didn't see herself filling that role, yet she couldn't escape the sense of responsibility she felt towards the young boy waiting for her.

In her mid-twenties, Chantal learned she would never be able to have children due to the toxic chemicals she had absorbed from bleaching. At first, the news did not bother her, but as time passed, knowing that she could never be a mother naturally greatly diminished her sense of her worth as a woman. Lost in thought, she placed her hand on her flat stomach, wishing she could rewind time and do research before inflicting irreversible harm to her body.

The driver announced once more that she had reached her destination, snapping her out of her thoughts. Glancing out the rear window, she saw a banner suspended above the entrance to the building, with large, bold letters spelling JCCA. After grabbing her purse and briefcase from the seat beside her, she cautiously stepped out of the car.

Although she typically appeared to be a very confident woman to those observing from the outside, Chantal entered JCCA filled with doubt and at a loss for words. She knew Jeremiah wanted to see her, having received countless letters from him. She managed to read the first two but then refused to read any more as guilt consumed her. She had a right to live her own life, yet she knew she should be doing more to help her nephew. Again, that was something she would never admit aloud, but she struggled with the feelings of knowing she had abandoned Jeremiah.

After signing in at the front desk and showing her ID, she was escorted to a small office to wait for Sandra. Glancing around, she noticed several photos on the walls of both children and adults; she assumed the adults were staff members. In one photograph, she spotted Jeremiah and got up to take a closer look. His solemn expression brought tears to her eyes, making her feel the need to do better by him. Just then, Sandra entered the room, and Chanel quickly sat back down. At first, Sandra seemed taken aback but then warmly introduced herself, extending her hand.

"Hello, Chantal. I'm Sandra Jacobs. It's nice to finally meet you."

As they exchanged greetings, Sandra couldn't help but notice the stark contrast between Chantal's light, faded complexion and Jeremiah's deep chocolate skin tone.

"Hello, Ms. Jacobs."

"Please, call me Sandra."

"Okay."

"Thank you for coming to see Jeremiah."

"Sure. So where is he?" Chantal asked, scanning the room as if she expected him to materialize out of thin air.

"I'll get him in a moment. I wanted to talk with you first."

Chantal kept glancing around anxiously, which led Sandra to say, "Jeremiah is truly a remarkable child, and I want nothing but the best for him."

"Well, we all want the best for him," Chantal countered, a bit defensively.

Noticing the shift in Chantal's tone, Sandra decided to quickly retrieve Jeremiah before the situation escalated further.

As Jeremiah walked into the room, Chantal gasped, struck by how much he resembled her as a child. She saw the sadness in his eyes, a reflection that took her years back to her own childhood memories.

Jeremiah was unsure why Ms. Jacobs wanted him to follow her, but he complied with her request. Sandra had not yet told him that the aunt he had been praying would come for him had arrived. When Jeremiah entered and saw Chantal, he did not immediately recognize her. She asked him to sit down while she continued to stare at him, struggling to hold back tears as sadness engulfed her.

"Jeremiah, do you know who this is?" Sandra asked gently.

Jeremiah looked at Chantal and slowly shook his head, confusion evident on his face. He had only seen her once in the past three years, and that encounter had been brief. Before that, it had been another two years. The bleaching had taken a serious toll on her skin, changing her so much that she was now almost unrecognizable.

"It's me...Chantal," she said, her voice trembling. "Your auntie, Jeremiah."

As Sandra observed their emotional exchange, she noticed a glimmer of hope in Jeremiah's eyes. She clasped her hands and brought them to her mouth, feeling a moment of gratitude for the fulfillment of a long-awaited promise.

Jeremiah was in disbelief. He glanced back and forth between Sandra and Chantal, overwhelmed with emotion. Then, without saying a word, he jumped up from the chair and wrapped his arms around Chantal's neck, holding her tightly as tears streamed down his cheeks. He silently thanked God for answering his prayers. In that heartfelt moment, Chantal also couldn't hold back her tears, weeping openly as she embraced Jeremiah and vowed to herself to care for her nephew, no matter the sacrifices it would require.

Wheel of Time
by Alicia J. Evans

"Making the very most of your time on earth, recognizing and taking advantage of each opportunity and using it with wisdom and diligence], because the days are [filled with] evil"
Ephesians 5:16

VANNA THROWS HER HEAD back as she swivels around in the large black leather chair to look out the window. Gazing at the New York City skyline always eases her tension and gives her a sense of calm, even if only for a moment. With her eyes closed, she attempts to pray away the impending migraine that threatens to ruin her day even more.

"What the hell happened?" she whispers in a strained voice to the empty office while massaging her temples to relieve the pressure of the migraine that disregarded her prayer.

Vanna inhales deeply and opens her eyes. When she accepted the marketing executive position at Simon &

Eva Tremaine & Alicia J. Evans

Schuster's main office in New York City, she had one requirement: she wanted an office with a breathtaking view of the vibrant city that never sleeps. As she looks out over the East Side, she starts to relax. Although the skyline has changed since the September 2011 terrorist attacks, the city is still captivating.

After earning her master's degree from Howard University, Vanna had no desire to return to her hometown of Queens. "Queens raised me, but Manhattan loves me," she would often say. Upon landing her job, the first thing she did was purchase a two-bedroom condo on the Upper West Side. The spacious open layout and floor-to-ceiling windows provided a dynamic view of the Empire State Building, the Chrysler Building, and the Grace Building. Each morning, she wakes to the view of the George Washington Bridge from her bedroom. Vanna's mother, a devoted native of Queens, struggled to understand her daughter's love for the bustling city. She often argued that Vanna could find an apartment in Long Island City with an equally impressive view of the Manhattan skyline.

The buzzing of the intercom abruptly interrupts Vanna's self-centering grounding time, alerting her that her assistant, Whitney, is on the other side of the closed door. Vanna slowly swivels her chair around and presses the incoming call button.

"Come on in," she says through the speaker, not giving Whitney a chance to reply.

Whitney and Vanna met during their freshman year at Howard University. They often joked that they were accidental roommates, brought together because Vanna's original upperclassman roommate didn't want to share a room with a freshman. Their bond formed from an unexpected circumstance, and they remained inseparable ever since.

Whitney did not have any family that she was aware of. Raised in the foster care system, she had no connection with relatives after her mother disappeared when she was five. In her senior year of high school, Whitney went on a mission to find her mother. The first thing she uncovered was that her mother had died from a drug overdose shortly after abandoning her at a local firehouse. The exact timing is unclear, as her body was found without identification and left unclaimed. She was buried on Hart Island in the Bronx, commonly known as Potter's Field. Utilizing the internet and Facebook, Whitney located an old friend of her mother who remembered Whitney when she was a baby. Through further research, Whitney learned that her mother was an only child whom her parents had given up for adoption, and to her dismay, those records were sealed. After graduating high school, she decided to set aside any pursuit of finding her biological family members.

While attending Howard University, Whitney spent the holidays on campus until Vanna found out. After that, she began going home with Vanna during the holidays and summer break. Whitney became the sister Vanna always wanted and a bonus daughter to Mr. and Mrs. Carlisle, Vanna's parents. People on campus often referred to them as sisters. Both women had small, petite frames, but their similarities ended there. Vanna had a round face with a reddish-brown complexion and dark freckles, whereas Whitney's face was long and oval-shaped, with a deep yellow tone featuring hints of brown. After graduating, they both enrolled in Howard's Master's program, and when Vanna received her job offer, she couldn't imagine working with anyone else but Whitney.

Whitney enters the office, pushing the door open with the force of a tornado. She drops a stack of files onto the coffee table and then walks over to Vanna's desk, her hands gliding over the rich mahogany surface before slowly trailing down to the drawers. When she reaches the third drawer from the top, she reaches in and pulls out the bottle of Tequila, all without saying a word.

As she watches her friend, Vanna arches her eyebrows and then relaxes them just as quickly. Whitney knows her well and is aware of where she keeps the booze. This was definitely the time for some Tequila, and of course, Vanna always has a bottle of her favorite, TCapri Tequila, in her desk drawer. It's her favorite not only because she loves the taste but also because it is the first Tequila brand owned by a Black woman.

"I'm not sure what happened with the Cummings case, but I do know we will fix it," Whitney says while pouring two shots of Tequila.

Vanna downs the shot, feeling the hint of caramel and vanilla begin to warm her chest.

"I'm not upset about the work. Well, not really. I'm more upset about the fact that it wasn't caught before today—today of all days when I really can't afford to stay late. In fact, my plan was to leave early," Vanna replies as she pours them another shot.

While some might find it odd to drink in the middle of the day during working hours, Vanna is quick to silence any talk by pointing out that the white male company executives sip on whiskey throughout the day in their offices without anyone commenting on it. Tequila shots have been their thing since college, and Vanna always has at least three bottles on hand. "A good shot of Tequila feels like a warm hug from your best friend," she always says.

Vanna is particular about her Tequila and serves only Black-owned brands to her colleagues. Since she and

Whitney are the only two women of color in their department, she believes it is important for them to represent their culture at every opportunity. So, whenever she calls a meeting with co-workers or clients, she ensures they taste the finest—and perhaps the only—Black-owned Tequila they will ever experience.

As she throws back her second shot, Vanna recalls her mother encouraging her to feed them Black every time. "Stay Black and proud!" her mother would often tell her.

"That's right. This weekend is the anniversary of Mrs. Margret's passing," Whitney says apologetically, snapping Vanna back to the present.

As Whitney speaks those words aloud, Vanna feels her ever-nagging migraine returning. She throws her head back and, with an exasperated grunt, flops into the chair across from Whitney. Due to her hectic work schedule trying to acquire Mr. Cummings' new book, Vanna and her daughter, Misty, have been like ships passing in the night. So, Vanna was looking forward to spending time with her teenage daughter, reminiscing as they shared memories of her mom and doing some of her favorite things.

Vanna glances at her watch, which feels like a brick on her wrist. She's late, and her driver is already downstairs. Rising from her chair, she pours one last shot of Tequila for both of them before putting the bottle back in her desk drawer. Then, closing her eyes, she inhales deeply and slowly exhales as she takes a sip, savoring its smoothness. After opening her eyes, she looks over at the files. Vanna knows if she delves into trying to figure out what went wrong, or rather, who fucked up, she will not get out of the office at a decent hour.

"Girl, this couldn't have happened at a worse time. Misty has been struggling this past year; her grades have dropped, and she withdrew from her mentorship program. I planned to spend this weekend reconnecting with my daughter and helping her cope with my momma's absence."

Whitney stood up from the sofa and walked over to her friend of more than twenty years, pulling her into a comforting hug and letting Vanna cry softly on her shoulder. Whitney understood that the weekend wasn't just for Misty; Vanna needed it, too.

Mrs. Margret, Vanna's mother, passed away after a long battle with cancer. She lived with Vanna and Misty during the last three years of her life. Before Mrs. Margret moved in with them, Misty would spend weekends and summers with her nana in Queens. This weekend marks the anniversary of Mrs. Margret's passing, and Vanna wants to prepare her mother's favorite dishes and enjoy her favorite shows with Misty.

"Listen, go home and start your weekend with Misty.

I'll pull an all-nighter and even come in tomorrow if I have to. I promise you, Vanna, I will find out exactly what happened and still be there early Sunday morning for breakfast. You're making your mother's famous buttermilk biscuits, right?" Whitney asks anxiously, silently pleading with her eyes.

Wiping away her tears, Vanna chuckles and replies, "Yes, Mama's biscuits will be on the menu."

* * *

If there was ever a time Vanna was grateful for a private car service to and from work, it was today. She sat in the back of the Cadillac Escalade, her head resting against the seat as she thought about her mother. This year had gone by so fast. Vanna felt a tug at her heart, sensing she had been shortchanged in their time together. It was the weekends spent with her mother during her childhood that she missed the most. During those weekends, her mother passed down the traditions she had shared with her own mother, Vanna's grandmother. Vanna's father understood the importance of their weekend mother-daughter time, so he would either go on a fishing trip with Vanna's uncles or hang out at one of his brothers' homes.

The crosstown traffic was horrendous on Fridays,

hence Vanna's reasoning for wanting to leave work early. Looking out the window, she rolls her eyes, thankful once again for not having to drive in this mess. To make use of her idle time, she takes out her phone and starts an Instacart order—one from Trader Joe's and another from Whole Foods. She schedules both deliveries for early the next morning. They didn't need anything tonight because, to kick off their weekend in memory of her mother, she would be ordering Chinese food, her mother's favorite, for their Friday night dinner and game night.

It amazes Vanna how the simple thought of ordering Chinese food triggers memories of her mother. After cooking all week, her mother often said, "There's a method to my madness," which was her way of explaining the logic behind spending less time in the kitchen and more time playing Spades or Crazy Eights on Friday nights. Vanna's eyes began to burn. She didn't want to cry because she knew that once the waterworks started, it would be hard to turn them off. Pulling a tissue from the dispenser in the armrest, Vanna dabs at the corners of her eyes. Thinking about her mother reminded her that it was the little things she did or said that always made her feel loved.

In an attempt to be in the present and stop going down memory lane, Vanna shifts her focus to Jimmy, her driver.

"Jimmy, the traffic this Friday afternoon is terrible, isn't it?"

"Yes, ma'am, it is."

Vanna glances at the rearview mirror and meets Jimmy's gaze. She nods and smiles as he winks and grins in return. Jimmy has been Vanna's personal driver for ten years. She hadn't realized she needed a driver until she had one.

Pulling out her phone again, she types a quick message to Whitney to check on things. She also texts Misty to let her know she's on her way home and will order Chinese once she gets there.

Once Jimmy parks in front of Vanna's building, she exits the vehicle, bids him goodnight, and wishes him a wonderful weekend. Before walking away, she quickly reminds him that he doesn't need to pick her up on Monday because she is taking the day off.

* * *

Now refreshed from her shower, Vanna sends another text to Whitney to express her gratitude, letting her know that she owes her big-time. She chuckles as she realizes that Whitney has truly been her sister from another mother since day one. She's not sure how she would have made it through some of life's trials without Whitney having her back. It was Whitney who stood beside her in the doctor's office when Dr. Tutu delivered the news of her mother's diagnosis. It was Whitney who comforted her when she collapsed to the floor, crying out in anguish after her mother took her final breath. And it was also Whitney who cradled her and Misty on the day of Mrs. Margret's funeral, rocking them for what felt like hours as they sat in the front pew of the church. With a smile, Vanna leaves her bedroom, knowing she can trust Whitney to fix the problem at work without her.

As Vanna enters the kitchen searching for the take-out menu from the Chinese restaurant, she calls out to Misty. When Vanna had arrived home, she peeked in on Misty, who, as usual, was absorbed in her phone. Vanna suspected it was either TikTok or Instagram that had her attention. She also thought her daughter might be using her phone to avoid talking to her.

After yelling down the hall three times for Misty and getting no response, Vanna decided to try a different method of communication. She sent her a text message: *What would you like me to order from the Chinese restaurant? And you know the drill. Come to the kitchen. NO phone.*

As soon as she hits the send arrow, Vanna realizes the mistake she made. Her child is a creature of habit and doesn't stray too far from her normal routine. Asking her what she wanted for dinner strongly suggested that she wasn't paying attention to her own child, which is far from the truth, but she knew Misty wouldn't see it that way.

* * *

Misty, in typical teenage fashion, hears her mother when she arrives home. She quickly puts on her Beats noise-canceling headphones. It doesn't matter that she hasn't connected them to her phone; she is simply using them as a decoy. She knows that as soon as her mother comes into the house, she will check on her.

The condo's two bedrooms are positioned at opposite ends of the unit, with Misty's room nearest to the front door. This means her mother has to pass by on her way to her own room. When Vanna stops to peek inside, Misty pretends to be engrossed in her phone. Once her mother closes the door, Misty rolls onto her back, staring at the ceiling and wishing her nana were still with them. Not knowing what else to do, she texts her father and prays he won't take long to reply.

Hey, Dad. When are you coming home?

After sending the message, Misty reflects on her parents' relationship. They aren't married, but they are together, and even though they lead separate lives, her father calls this place home. They profess their love for one another, yet they do not allow their relationship to interfere with their careers. As it was explained to Misty, Patrick, her father, had always aspired to be a traveling doctor, wanting to care for the less fortunate, but he believed that bouncing from place to place was not a suitable way to raise a daughter. Her mother, on the other hand, had dreamed of launching a Black women-owned publishing house one day and felt she could not achieve her goal if she was constantly relocating every few months.

Misty looks down at her phone and, noticing her dad hasn't replied, disappointingly tosses it to the foot of the bed and shrugs. She then jumps up and heads to the kitchen to join her mother. As Misty enters, she overhears the end of her mother's phone conversation. Instantly, she gets an attitude since her mother always preaches about no phones in the kitchen, yet here she is on a call. Without any effort to hide her disdain, Misty rolls her eyes and sucks her teeth. She immediately regrets it when she realizes her mother is talking to her father.

"I love you, too. Travel safely, and I will see you when you get home. I'll let Misty know you will be here on Sunday morning."

Misty can't hear her father's response on the other end, but judging by her mother's expression, she's sure it's something sweet. When she hears Misty giggling, Vanna quickly turns around, her face flushed with embarrassment. Amused by her mother's guilty look, Misty begins to back out of the kitchen. However, she stops in her tracks when Vanna shakes her finger in her direction, signaling her not to leave.

"Misty just came in the kitchen," Vanna says and then passes her the phone.

Taking the phone from her mother, Misty begins to feel better just hearing her father's deep baritone voice. After he apologizes for not responding to her text, he promises to be home on Sunday and assures her that he won't miss breakfast. Feeling somewhat better, Misty ends the call and hands the phone back to her mother. Vanna takes the phone and smiles as she opens a drawer to place it inside, giving her daughter a look that conveys her understanding that the rules apply to her, too.

"Oh, and by the way, the next time you suck your teeth in my house, I can guarantee I will knock those same teeth out of your mouth," Vanna sternly expresses, making it clear that disrespect will not be tolerated.

Misty looks at her mother solemnly; she didn't mean to upset her. Misty had assumed her mother was so absorbed in the phone conversation that she hadn't heard her, but she was wrong. Acknowledging her mistake, Misty begins pulling dishes from the cabinet to set the table for dinner.

Her nana always talked to her about respecting her parents. Eye-rolling, teeth-sucking, and backtalk were all considered disrespectful, and her nana taught her better. She would also remind Misty that mothers have eyes and ears everywhere.

How could I forget that? Misty thinks to herself as she shakes her head and giggles at her own forgetfulness.

While sitting at the table eating their Chinese food, Vanna attempts to make small talk with her daughter.

"How was your day, honey?"

"Fine"

"How did you do on your math quiz?"

"Ok."

"What grade did you get on your science project?"

Vanna is sure that this question will elicit more than just a one-word response. If she knows anything about her daughter, it's that she loves science—something Misty inherited from her father and not Vanna.

"An A."

Vanna gazes sorrowfully at her daughter, lays her fork down, and slowly reaches for her glass of wine. After taking a long, slow sip, she places the glass back down while continuing to look at her child. She watches as Misty pushes the food from one side of the plate to the other, hardly eating at all. Occasionally, Misty takes a

81

small forkful of food and chews it. Vanna understands that her daughter misses her nana. She feels the same but knows she needs to help her child cope with their loss. The question is, how?

When Margret fell ill, Vanna and Patrick agreed that it would be better for Misty not to know. They believed she was too young to handle such devastating news. Looking at her daughter now, Vanna questions whether they made the right decision years ago. Maybe they should have told her instead of moving Margret in with them and allowing Misty to witness the rapid decline of her health. And still, they did not tell her until it was quite obvious that Margret was not getting any better.

"Penny for your thoughts."

Vanna silently prays this will work. It's something her mother used to say when it was too quiet at the dinner table.

After what feels like an eternity, Misty responds, "Why do I always order Pepper Steak? You can count on one hand the amount of steak they put in here. Instead, they should call it Peppers and Onions with a hint of steak."

They start laughing, recalling Margret saying those exact words every time she ordered Pepper Steak.

Finally, the mood has shifted. Smiling, Misty looks at her mother and begins to reminisce about the time her nana took her on her first bus ride to Main Street in Flushing, also known as Chinatown, in Queens.

"Baby, there's Queens College. Nana's gonna make sure you go there when you're ready for college. Me and your poppa went there. As a matter of fact, that's where we met," Misty recalls her nana saying as the Q17 bus made a right turn onto Kissena Boulevard.

Getting emotional, Misty looks up to see her mother looking back at her, and what she sees stirs something deep inside her. Her mother's eyes gleam with eagerness; she wants to hear more—no, she needs to hear more. Savoring this moment, Misty recounts the day her nana was so excited to show her the Queens Botanical Garden.

"Look, baby, there's the Queens Botanical Garden. I'ma take you there for the flower show one day. I bet you ain't never seen anything like it," Misty says, trying to mimic her nana's voice.

Misty closes her eyes, recalling her nana's gentle voice and the scent of Palmer's Cocoa Butter lotion on her skin. When she opens her eyes again, Misty stares at her mother. It's hard for her to picture her mother as a young girl.

With dinner finished and the dishwasher loaded, Vanna searches through the movie bin for one of her mother's favorite films for their movie night. They had decided on movies for this Friday evening instead of games. While Misty is in the kitchen making popcorn, Vanna selects a collection of *Wheel of Fortune* game show recordings. Though not a movie, it will do.

Vanna recalls the Christmas when they gifted her mother the DVD collection. Margret was astonished by the array of recordings on the DVDs. Thanks to Patrick's friend converting the VCR tapes into DVDs, her mother could enjoy her recordings for years to come, especially since video cassette players were no longer manufactured.

After two bowls of popcorn and three hours of Vanna White and Pat Sajak, Misty turns to her mother and says, "Tell me about your name again."

With slight hesitation, Vanna reaches for her now-empty wine glass. Without the warm, bubbly Moscato to tickle her throat, she slowly swallows her unease as she begins to share the story of the origin of her name, which she is sure Misty has heard a thousand times.

"It was the Saturday of a holiday weekend, and ABC was running a twenty-four-hour *Wheel of Fortune* special. Nana had been having stomach cramps all day but didn't want to tell Pops because she knew he would insist on taking her to the hospital. So, after Pops went to work, Nana stayed in bed all day watching Pat and Vanna while drinking hot tea."

In the dim light of the now muted television, Vanna reaches out to locate the box of Kleenex tissues. Recalling the story she has heard countless times, she thinks about how her mother used to imitate Vanna White as she turned those illuminated cubes to uncover the secret word or phrase. As she twists and tears a tissue, she swallows the lump that has formed in her throat, struggling to mask the emotions starting to cloud the joy she should feel while sharing the story.

"When Pops returned home that evening, he found Nana on the floor with my head peeking from between her legs."

As they both laugh, the cloud lifts, and Vanna is able to enjoy the rest of the evening with her daughter.

* * *

"Alexa, play James Cleveland," Vanna commands her Echo Dot.

Not feeling quite ready to get out of bed just yet, she decides it won't hurt to lie there for an extra twenty minutes and bask in the afterglow of Patrick's call confirming he will be home before noon. She feels happy that her man will be home and that Misty will get to spend time with her dad.

Thinking back over the weekend, she couldn't be happier with how it was shaping up. Friday night ended with her and Misty both falling asleep on the sofa, and

Saturday was spent cleaning and reconnecting with her daughter. She managed to convince Misty to enroll in the mentorship program and promised her that she would hire a tutor to help her get back on track with her studies. Lastly, with Whitney finally getting to the bottom of the issues with the Cummings' account on Saturday morning, Vanna could fully focus on making the remainder of her mother's one-year death anniversary perfect for everyone.

When her mother was alive, Sunday mornings were all about gospel music and church. Although Vanna didn't regularly attend church once she got older, she never forgot her upbringing. If she were honest with herself, she would admit that she missed the feeling of Sunday mornings from her childhood. After her mother passed away, going to church or playing gospel music became too painful for her. However, this morning, she wanted to feel her mother's presence in her home. She also silently promised she would start attending church again.

Listening to Reverend James Cleveland always reminded her of her childhood, when his music played in the background every Sunday while her mother cooked in the kitchen—the aroma of Maxwell House coffee and bacon wafting upstairs to her bedroom.

Vanna pulls the duvet over her head and sinks deeper

into the bed. She wants to give herself this time because she won't allow herself to break down in front of Misty. Suddenly, Vanna throws back the covers, sits up in bed, and inhales slowly. Shaking her head, she inhales again, this time much deeper.

"Is that bacon and coffee? Nah, it can't be."

Curious to see if her mind is playing tricks on her, Vanna gets out of bed, puts on her robe, and walks down the hallway to the kitchen. What she finds upon entering takes her breath away.

With her headphones on, Misty stirs pots while softly singing the words to "Lord Help Me to Hold Out", just like her nana used to. Leaning against the wall for support, Vanna silently cries and smiles as she watches her child. In this moment, she realizes that the decision she and Patrick made for Misty to spend weekends with her parents is one they can be proud of.

Misty woke up thinking about her nana. She knew her mother had planned to prepare a big breakfast/brunch to celebrate her nana. Her dad had promised to return home in time for breakfast, and she knew her godmother, Aunt Whitney, would be joining them. After their bonding time this weekend, Misty realized that her mother was hurting, too, and she shouldn't have made this time any harder for her. It had been a rough year for both of them, and she promised to do better.

As Misty turns around to get the buttermilk from the refrigerator, she notices her mother standing there, watching her. Removing her headphones, she walks over to her mother's open arms.

Hugging her daughter, Vanna says, "It smells good in here."

"Thank you, Ma," Misty responds as she goes to the refrigerator to collect the items she needs.

With gospel music continuing to play in the background, the kitchen comes alive as Vanna and Misty move about preparing dishes and engaging in light conversation.

Momma would be proud, Vanna thinks to herself.

Once everyone arrives and is seated at the table, Vanna glances around at the people she loves: Patrick, Misty, and Whitney. She then lifts her glass to make a toast.

"The wheel of time is like life. You must keep going. The wheel goes 'round and doesn't allow anything to stop it. Momma always said not to let the wheel of time stop on your life. Keep moving."

Raising her glass higher and speaking with a labored voice while fighting back her tears, Vanna concludes the toast with a promise to her mother.

"Momma, we're going to keep moving the wheel."

The Weight of Silence
by Eva Tremaine

Silence can be more lethal than any spoken word.

MIA STOOD BEFORE THE mirror, admiring her flawless reflection. A cascade of chestnut hair framed her delicate face, and her eyes—deep brown and bright with the promise of success—seemed to hold the entire world's expectations. On the outside, she radiated perfection—beautiful, intelligent, and well-liked. She was the girl others envied, the one praised by teachers, the one destined for greatness. She ranked at the top of her class, was the captain of the debate team, and volunteered at the local shelter. With a bright future ahead, she had her whole life to look forward to.

However, inside, Mia was crumbling.

A storm swirled beneath her poised demeanor, concealed behind her practiced smiles and rehearsed laughter. She harbored a secret, one so dark it felt like a weight pressing down on her heart and crushing her soul. She had worked so hard to appear unbreakable, but the effort it took to keep up the façade was exhausting. Yet, she had vowed to take the secret to her grave, convinced that if anyone found out, it would shatter her family, leaving devastation and shame in its wake.

The secret gnawed at her mind constantly, consuming her thoughts day and night. She tried to push it away, telling herself she could handle it and that it would disappear with time. However, as the months passed, the burden only grew heavier, its weight becoming increasingly unbearable. The guilt felt suffocating, and the fear of anyone discovering the truth was paralyzing. She navigated through her days wearing a mask of perfection while internally drowning in the silence of her pain.

Mia was loved by both family and friends, but no one saw beyond her perfect exterior. No one noticed the cracks forming beneath the surface, threatening to break her. Her mother, always busy with work, regarded Mia as her shining star. Her father, strict yet loving, often told her how proud he was of her achievements. Then there was her younger brother, Michael, who idolized her. To everyone around her, Mia was the epitome of success and everything good and right in the world.

But they didn't know. They couldn't know.

One evening, after another day of smiling, pretending,

and bearing the weight of her secret, Mia sat on her bed, staring at the four walls of her room. They felt as though they were closing in on her, compressing her world with unbearable pressure. She could feel her heart racing, her throat tightening, and her breath coming in shallow gasps. Tears welled in her eyes, blurring her vision, but she didn't bother to wipe them away.

It was too much. The silence was deafening, the burden too great. She couldn't keep living like this. She couldn't keep pretending everything was fine when every moment felt like a battle to keep the darkness from swallowing her whole. She promised herself that she wouldn't let it happen again, but there she was, sitting in shame, reflecting on yesterday and what they had done.

In that moment, Mia made a decision. She would find peace in the only way she believed possible. That night, Mia ended her life. She swallowed pill after pill, choking while getting the lethal dose down. Then, it was done. She succumbed to her pain.

The news hit her family like a hurricane, ripping through their lives without warning. How could this have happened? Mia had everything—a bright future, love, and opportunities that others would kill for. She was their golden girl, the one who had always seemed so sure of herself. Their grief was immeasurable, but what haunted them the most was the lingering question: Why?

They searched her room for answers, desperate to understand. They combed through her belongings—her trophies, certificates, photos with friends, and neatly stacked textbooks—all evidence of a life filled with promise, yet none of it explained why she had chosen to leave them. It seemed nothing could explain the darkness she had kept hidden.

Until Michael found her diary.

Hidden in the bottom drawer of her dresser, beneath clothes she no longer wore, was the diary. Its pages were worn, with ink smudged in places where her tears had fallen. Michael spent countless hours in Mia's room, seeking comfort in the space she once occupied, trying to feel her presence. He would sit there, talking to her, sharing his day, struggling to cope with the loss of his sister. At first, he didn't realize what he had found. His hands trembled as he picked up the diary, uncertain if he should open it—unsure if he could face what it held. But he had to know.

With a heavy heart, he turned the pages, each word pulling him deeper into his sister's world. In her neat, flowing script, Mia wrote of the guilt and shame that consumed her. A betrayal—something unspeakable that had happened to her, an unforgivable act that broke her from within. She had been hurt, trapped, and terrified. And the one person who could have stopped it, the one person who should have protected her, had failed her.

Michael's breath caught in his throat as he read the words. His hands trembled, causing the diary to slip from his grasp and fall to the floor with a soft thud. He couldn't believe it. How had he not seen it? How had she carried this burden alone for so long?

The truth she had taken such great care to hide was now laid before him, its weight suffocating. Mia's silence—the silence that had destroyed her—was now his to bear. The secret she thought would die with her was now his to keep.

He stared at the pages scattered on the floor, his heart aching from the realization that he had failed her, too. He had idolized her but hadn't truly seen her. He hadn't seen her pain or noticed the subtle cries for help concealed behind her smiles.

But the words couldn't be real. He wept, desperate for them to be false. Yet, as he read Mia's painful secret in her handwriting, he knew this unbearable truth had been her reality. Stunned and devastated, he sat there, unsure of what to do. He understood why Mia kept it hidden, but the weight of her silence had ultimately consumed her.

Michael sat for hours, consumed by every painful detail, with fury building with each discovery. Day turned to night, but he couldn't move, paralyzed by the tragedy of unspoken words. As moonlight filtered through the window, casting shadows on the walls, he came to a grim realization: no matter what he did now, the burden of silence had already passed from her to him. Now it was his to bear.

With unimaginable restraint, Michael kept the secret until the following day. Her death would not be in vain.

As he entered the living room, his family sat gathered—his mother, father, aunt, two cousins, and grandmother. Michael walked in with the diary clutched tightly in his hand and made his way directly to his father. Tears welled in his eyes as he approached, and with trembling hands, he threw the diary at his father's feet. The words that had been burning inside him, threatening to consume him, finally broke free.

"How could you?!" His voice cracked, raw and full of anguish. "How could you do that to her?"

The room fell silent. His mother and grandmother exchanged bewildered glances while his father sat in shock, narrowing his eyes.

"Do what to who, son?"

His father's voice was calm, but the slight twitch in his jaw revealed his unease.

Michael's chest heaved as rage and sorrow twisted inside him.

"It's all in her diary!" he shouted, pointing at his

father. "You! You're the reason she's gone! You did this to Mia. She couldn't take it anymore because of what you were doing to her."

His words sliced through the silence like a knife.

His father blinked, a wave of confusion washing over his face.

"Son, what are you saying?"

Michael could feel the weight of his family's stares, but he refused to meet their gazes. His focus remained on the man in front of him—the man he had once admired but now viewed in an entirely different light.

"It's your fault!" Michael screamed, his voice hoarse and trembling. "She wrote everything. She couldn't tell anyone because she was terrified, because you made her feel like she had no choice. You were raping her, Dad. It's all in here." He pointed to the scattered pages, his voice faltering as the gravity of his words pressed down on him.

The room erupted in chaos. His mother gasped, covering her mouth, while his aunt stood up, her face pale with disbelief. His father remained seated while staring at the floor, refusing to meet anyone's gaze. Suddenly, his father's expression twisted with anger.

"That's not true!" he shouted, his voice defensive and rising with fury. "I don't know what she wrote in that diary, but I never did anything like that! She was my daughter! How could you accuse me of something so vile?"

Michael's certainty wavered for a moment, doubt creeping in. But then he remembered the raw pain in Mia's words—the pain she had carried alone, the pain she had been too afraid to speak aloud.

"She's not here to defend herself," Michael said, his voice quieter yet resolute. "She was too scared to tell anyone, but I'm here to speak for her."

Tears streamed down his face as the room erupted with shouts of denial and cries of disbelief—but none of it reached him. Michael had spoken the truth. It shattered the world he had known, but something inside him felt lighter. The burden of silence, which had weighed so heavily on him since the moment he opened Mia's diary, had been lifted.

In that moment, amidst the chaos and a shattered family, Michael realized that the weight of Mia's silence no longer belonged to him alone. He had freed her voice, and in doing so, he had freed himself from the crushing weight that had threatened to destroy him. As the silence broke, he felt Mia's love envelop him, her truth finally released.

Behind the Veil
by Alicia J. Evans

Veil: a covering or protection

LILLIAN SAT WITH HER 4-inch Louboutin heels impatiently tapping the footrail of the barstool.

Rolling her eyes and blowing out an exasperated breath, she asked herself, *Why did Nicole insist I meet her here?*

Lillian looked around and noticed the men in their hoodies and Timbs posted up on one side of the bar while the women in leggings and UGGs sat at tables. Feeling out of place, Lillian tugged at her Ralph Lauren blazer and pulled her Louis Vuitton tote closer to her chest. She prayed Nicole had a good reason for insisting they meet at this neighborhood dive.

"Meet me at five o'clock, please," she had pleaded before ending the call without waiting for a reply.

Had she given Lillian a minute to respond, Lillian would have shared a million reasons why she couldn't meet with her. Starting with the fact that she was stuck in a meeting, her clients were uncooperative, and she had a dinner date. Okay, the last one was really a stretch, but hey, Lillian thought she would give it her best shot.

The Bar in the Hood was located on South Road, right in the heart of Southside Jamaica. Over the years, several owners attempted to change the ambience to reflect the area's gentrification, but to their dismay, the clientele stayed the same. Fancy drinks and delicate dishes were not what the Southside desired. Cold beer, wings, greasy fries, and large-screen TVs made the place feel just right for the neighborhood.

Digging into her Louis Vuitton tote, Lillian blindly searched for her phone, again wondering what was keeping Nicole. She began to think the worst. *Maybe she was involved in an accident. What if she got shot while at work?* Lillian hated that Nicole was a homicide detective with the New York City Police Department. Lillian's hands began to shake, and she absentmindedly picked up a napkin to occupy her hands as she started to panic. She did not think she could go on if she lost Nicole, too.

Lillian and Nicole had been friends for over fifteen years. A college frat party brought them together. Lillian never liked going to those things, but she went to keep an eye on her freshman roomie, Chance. She felt alcohol, weed, and young people were never a good combination. But with it being her senior year, she decided to go out and live a little.

It was around two o'clock in the morning, and she was more than ready to call it a night. She could not wait to get back to her dorm to wash the awful smell of weed and cigarettes out of her hair and off her body. After searching and not being able to locate Chance, Lillian began to panic, moving from room to room with urgency. She apologized for interrupting groups of college students engaged in sexual activities and cautiously stepped over intoxicated classmates who were celebrating their first real night of freedom by saying yes to everything offered to them. Lillian's eyes darted from face to face, trying to recognize the freckle-faced, always-smiling Chance. She could feel the sweat on her forehead. Her breathing became labored, and everything around her was a blur.

How in the world did she lose sight of her roommate? Lillian had read stories about what happened at these parties, and she believed that attending with Chance was the best way to keep her safe. She messed up. Oh my God, how will I ever explain this to her parents? Lillian thought as she fell to her knees, devastated. This is how she would be remembered in her last year at Howard University: the person who lost her roommate.

"Hey...hey...you looking for Chance?" Lillian heard a strange voice ask. "She told me to let you know she was leaving and going back to the dorm."

Still feeling a bit woozy, Lillian wasn't sure she had heard *the girl correctly.*

Reaching down, the stranger helped Lillian off the floor.

"Here, let me help you up. Damn, you spiral quick," the stranger mumbled, laughing while balancing a red Solo cup with her teeth.

Lillian got to her feet and wiped crushed potato chips and whatever else was on the floor off of her pants.

"Here, take this. You seem to need it more than I do."

The strange young woman extended the cup she had taken from the grip of her front teeth to Lillian.

"Uh, no thank you," Lillian replied while backing away, then thought to herself, Why in the hell would I take a drink from her? The first two things you learn about partying are to never accept a drink from a stranger and to leave with who you came with. Where the hell is Chance?

"I'm sorry, girl. I'm Nicole," the stranger replied with a giggle. Then, pushing the cup toward Lillian, she added, "This is just water. I never drink at these parties. I carry the red cup so everyone thinks it's liquor. Someone needs to be sober in case they need to be designated to do something. By the way, Chance said she looked for you and couldn't find you, so she bounced. I was across the room when I spotted you from the description Chance gave me. I noticed the panicked look on your face, but then you went down."

Nicole stood there, still pushing the cup in her face. Lillian took the cup but didn't drink from it. She didn't quite trust this

Nicole person, whom she didn't know from Adam.

That night marked the beginning of their sisterhood. Lillian later learned that Nicole and Chance had grown up in the same neighborhood in Queens. Lillian was now part of their friendship circle.

Lillian instinctively glanced from the front door back to her phone, growing more upset as the clock ticked away. She ran her fingers along the shiny wood bar top, which was coated with a sticky residue from years of drink spills.

There isn't enough Pledge in the world to remove this grime, she thought.

Looking down at the wood floor, which bore the marks of countless nights filled with The Cuban Shuffle and Cha-Cha Slide line dances, a wave of familiarity washed over her. Shrugging it off, Lillian laughed. This wasn't her kind of spot, but Chance and Nicole would absolutely love it here.

"Can I get you something while you wait?"

Lillian smiled as pleasantly as she could at the bartender, who she was sure was annoyed that she had been occupying the same stool for the past hour without ordering a drink. Taking the plastic drink menu in hand, she examined both the front and back, perpetrating a fraud. It didn't matter what was on the menu or what the Happy Hour specials were; she was ordering a martini.

Her only dilemma was what flavor. Her choice always depended on her mood. Was she in the mood for apple, chocolate, or watermelon? Or maybe she would switch it up and order a mango martini.

Looking up at the bulked-up bartender, she chuckled to herself, thinking, *He probably doesn't even know how to make a damn martini.*

"Can you make a chocolate martini with Tito's?"

With a toothpick dangling from the side of his mouth, the bartender leaned across the wooden bar, smiled, and replied, "I think I can do that."

Before walking away, he stared at Lillian for what she felt was a little too long. It was as if he was dissecting her with a fine-toothed comb. Maybe he recognized her from somewhere, but she doubted it. Lillian grew up in Hempstead, Long Island, and even though the bar was about a thirty-five-minute drive from her hometown, she never ventured to this part of Jamaica, Queens. Before she could let him know she didn't appreciate him eyeballing her, he was gone to fix her drink.

Shifting in her seat, she fumbled to retrieve her phone. After finally locating it, she checked her text messages to see if Nicole had sent an explanation for her delay. Finding nothing from Nicole, she quickly scanned her contacts and called her instead.

While waiting for the call to connect, Lillian reminisced

about one of their many girls' nights out...

"Girl, you always ordering a martini. Then you get mad at the bartender when they don't make it correctly," Nicole said while shaking her head and rolling her eyes.

In Lillian's own defense, she retorted, *"How hard is it to make a martini? Not very hard. There are only three to five ingredients. Simple, right?"*

Lillian stood her ground on why every bartender should know how to make a martini.

Lillian stifled a laugh as she remembered that particular girls' night out with Nicole and Chance. She always had a good time when they hung out.

Still waiting for Nicole to answer, Lillian felt bad that they had allowed life to get in the way of their time together. All three were successful and worked hard to maintain their chosen careers while balancing family responsibilities. Excuse after excuse, one missed date after another. It turned into months, and then years went by without them getting together. Phone calls and text messages quickly filled the void. The generic form of communication was easy.

Solemnly, Lillian accepted that this past year, she had been the reason for the many rescheduled dates and ultimately canceling altogether on Nicole. Shrugging her shoulders, she tried to shake off the uncomfortable feeling she was experiencing.

"Perfect timing," she murmured as the bartender placed a round paper coaster in front of her and set the martini on top of it.

With that damn toothpick still dangling from the side of his mouth, he said, "Enjoy."

Stepping back and leaning against the wine refrigerator, he folded his muscular arms across his chest.

"Well?" he asked, nodding toward the drink Lillian had just set back down.

"Not bad," was all Lillian said.

In all actuality, Lillian wanted to tell him it was one hell of a martini. The shaved chocolate with the drizzled chocolate around the rim was the perfect touch. When Lillian didn't offer any other compliments, he walked away while grinning. Lillian couldn't resist the urge to check out the bartender's package from behind.

Mmmm. Lillian continued to stare at his backside while sipping her drink. *Okay, this is ridiculous,* she thought. *What the hell is keeping Nicole?*

Just as she was about to snatch her phone to call Nicole, it buzzed, signaling she had a text message.

Sorry. Running late. Order wings. Will be there soon.

Lillian was pissed. This was typical Nicole behavior. She would be late for her own funeral if it were up to her. Lillian laughed at the old folks' saying but realized it was definitely true when it came to Nicole. She looked for the bartender to ask about an order from the kitchen when she noticed him at the other end of the long bar.

"Damn, he's fine" Lillian whispered to herself.

Watching him interact with a young woman who looked to be more than half his age, Lillian felt a twinge of jealousy. Shaking it off, she succumbed to, *This is the story of my life.* Swallowing the last of her drink, she looked into the empty glass. Suddenly, her mood changed. *Empty—never allow yourself to feel empty* was Chance's favorite quote. She would write it at the end of every text message and use it to conclude every call. Chance often said, "Life is too short and full of too many wonderful things for you to feel empty inside."

Lillian usually had one drink when she had to drive, but tonight, she would make an exception. After all, what else was she supposed to do while waiting for Nicole? Finally getting the bartender's attention, she asked him for a menu.

Derrick, the bartender and owner, reluctantly handed Lillian the menu. He hoped the slight pause would give her time to recognize him. When Lillian walked into the bar, he was sure she was the woman who had been there a year ago at his homegirl Chance's memorial. To be certain, he asked his daughter if she also recognized the woman as Aunt Chance's friend. He would never forget the woman whose wails that day pierced his heart. Plus,

Chance always talked about her roommate from her freshman year at Howard University.

When there was no spark of recognition in Lillian's eyes, Derrick finally said, "May I suggest the wing platter? It's a sampling of all our best flavors. We also have salmon sliders, and our crispy Brussels sprouts are banging, I promise you."

Lillian quickly glanced through the menu and decided on her choices, but she refused to give in to him so easily.

"Do you have salad?" Lillian asked. "I don't see it on the menu."

"Yes, we have a taco salad, which is a garden salad served in a taco bowl. It's one of our most requested items, along with the wings."

Before Lillian could place her order, Bruno Mars' "Count on Me" ringtone alerted her that Nicole was calling.

"Excuse me," she said to the bartender while digging in her bag for her phone. "Girl, where are you? You know my bougie ass ain't comfortable, and you got me up in here by myself," Lillian rambled on, not letting Nicole get a word in.

"Dang, girl, slow down. My Uber is pulling up in front now. Did you get a booth?" Nicole shouted quickly.

"Wait, what? An Uber?" Lillian asked, her voice laced with concern.

"Lillian, you know I'm always the designated whatever. You and Chance were always getting your drink on. Someone had to make sure y'all got home safely," Nicole replied while getting out of the car. "I'm walking through the doors now. Hang up."

Turning around on her bar stool, Lillian let out a sigh of relief.

Finally, she turned to the bartender and said, "I'll have the wing sampler, the sliders, Brussels sprouts, taco salad, and another chocolate martini.

Nicole raced across the bar with two dozen balloons in Chance's favorite colors, blue and yellow. As Lillian watched her, she suddenly took in the entire atmosphere of the bar. Why hadn't she noticed it before? The same long wooden bar that was covered with baskets of sympathy flowers. The same floor covered with petals from the lilies that decorated one corner of the bar.

This can't be the place where we had Chance's memorial, is it? Lillian wondered as her eyes darted from one square inch to the next. Her breath caught in her throat. *It can't be.*

The round tables she would have remembered—and the booths. Surely, she wouldn't forget the day of Chance's memorial.

Nicole and Chance grew up in the Forty Projects, just a short distance from the bar. On the day Chance sat them down and shared her stage 4 breast cancer diagnosis with only months to live, the one thing she requested was that they hold her memorial in her childhood neighborhood. Chance loved her old neighborhood, and even after college, she returned to open and operate many organizations to give back to her community. How could Lillian forget something this important?

Lillian had blocked out everything about the day of Chance's funeral and memorial, including the date she passed away. Now, glancing over the bar, she noticed the many pictures on the wall. There were photos of Chance giving out turkeys for Thanksgiving and even one of Chance with the bartender standing in front of a large tractor-trailer filled with toys to be given out to the children in the community for Christmas. How had Lillian not noticed those pictures before?

Lillian recalled her therapist telling her that she copes by putting up a veil to mask or hide things that have caused her trauma. Her therapist described it to Lillian as repressed memories. Lillian buried the memory of Chance's passing so deep in her mind that she didn't remember the date or the bar. With the veil now lifted and memories of her sister-friend flooding back, she took hurried breaths as she realized what their dinner meeting today was truly about—to remember their friend.

No wonder Nicole insisted they meet here on this day—January fourteenth, a full year since Chance died. Lillian felt breathless. How could she forget Chance? Her heart ached all over again, and her knees felt weak. They wouldn't support her for long. It was then that Nicole released the balloons to the ceiling, and before Lillian could hit the floor, she pulled her in for a tight embrace.

As Lillian collapsed into Nicole's arms, grateful for the love of her friend, who had come to her aid once more when she needed her most, despite what today meant for her too, she heard their theme song blaring through the speakers. In unison, with tears streaming down their faces, they sang, "Thank you for being my friend."

Shots Fired
by Eva Tremaine

No one knows when their final moment will arrive.
Cherish each moment.

IN THE DIMLY LIT high school hallway, chaos erupted as screams echoed off lockers and students scattered at the sound of gunshots. The sharp crack of bullets sliced through the air, causing the lockers to rattle and nerves to fray. Students laughing and chatting in groups now found themselves gripped by sheer panic, their faces pale with terror as they ran in every direction, some stumbling and falling in their haste to flee.

Inside Classroom 103, a group of frightened students huddled together, their eyes widened with fear. A few courageous souls frantically assisted the teacher in pushing the desks and chairs against the door in a desperate attempt to barricade themselves inside. Once vibrant with colorful posters and neatly arranged desks, the classroom had transformed into a fortress, with the makeshift barriers serving as their only defense. An eerie silence filled the space, save for the ragged breathing of the students and the occasional sob from someone trying hard to contain their emotions.

Moments earlier, Alex had excused himself to go to the restroom down the hall. Once inside, he turned up the volume of the music streaming through his noise-canceling earbuds, leaving him oblivious to the pandemonium. It wasn't until he stepped out of the restroom that he realized something was horribly wrong. The hallway, usually bustling with activity, was now empty. The distant sounds of screams and gunfire were the only indications of the chaos unfolding nearby. Alex's heart raced, each beat pounding in his ears as he tried to steady his shaking hands. The once-familiar path to the restroom now felt like a labyrinth of danger, with every turn a possible hiding spot for the shooter.

The blaring sirens were accompanied by a series of announcements over the PA system, alerting students of an active shooter and instructing them to lockdown. Students followed the lockdown procedures, remaining silent and out of sight as they were taught. Franklin High School had practiced this drill multiple times, yet Alex's mind went blank in the face of real danger. His thoughts were jumbled as he struggled to recall what to do. Breathing in quick, panicked gasps, his legs felt like lead, refusing to carry him to the safety of a classroom.

In his state of panic, Alex's attention shifted to his phone, which he gripped tightly in his hand. The small device felt like a lifeline rather than just a constant companion in his daily life. Trembling uncontrollably, he decided to do the only thing he could think of—call his mother. His fingers fumbled over the screen as he dialed her number. When she picked up, her warm, soothing voice starkly contrasted with the terror surrounding him.

"Mom..." Alex's voice cracked, tears welling in his eyes as he struggled to get the words out. "There's...there's a shooter. I don't know what to do."

Typically a fun-loving and confident teenager, Alex now felt uncertainty and fear. At fifteen, he was a sophomore at Franklin High School, a place that usually made him feel safe and happy. He enjoyed playing basketball with his friends, cracking jokes that made everyone laugh, and hanging out on the court after school. As the only child of Katherine and Johnathan Robinson, they had always been his pillars of strength. While his father often took on the role of disciplinarian, his mother provided him with love and a sense of security.

On the other end of the line, his mother's voice instantly shifted to one of calm urgency. The fear in her heart was masked by her need to stay strong for her son.

"Alex, listen to me. Find somewhere to hide and lock the door if you can. Stay quiet; don't make a sound. I'm coming, okay? I'm coming to get you."

Alex's mother had been at home, enjoying a peaceful afternoon watching television. The tranquility of her day was abruptly shattered when a news alert flashed across the screen—*New Brunswick, New Jersey: Active Shooter at Franklin High School.* The chilling words made her heart skip a beat as fear tightened its hold on her. She sat there frozen in shock, her mind struggling to process this horrifying reality. Her hands trembled as she fumbled for the remote, cranking the volume to the highest level, desperate to catch every word. The news anchor's voice, though calm, was infused with urgency as more details emerged.

"We have confirmed reports of an active shooter inside Franklin High School. The shooter's identity remains unknown at this time, and authorities have not reported any fatalities. Police and hostage negotiators are on the scene, working to bring the situation under control."

Alex's mother could barely breathe as she listened, her thoughts spiraling into panic. *Is Alex safe? What if there's a shootout between the shooter and the police, and my son gets caught in the crossfire?* The uncertainty gnawed at her as each second stretched into an agonizing eternity.

She wanted to take action, to do something, but all she could do was wait — wait for more news, wait for a phone call, wait for any sign that her child was okay. Authorities had urged parents not to come to the school or try to call their children, warning that doing so might alert the shooter to their hiding places. However, after receiving a call from her son, the thought of sitting there idle became unbearable.

Ignoring the warning, Alex's mother snatched her keys from the foyer table and rushed out the door, fueled by adrenaline. As she sped toward the school, her hands shook despite her firm grip on the steering wheel. She thought about calling her husband but worried that if she tried to add him to the call, she might lose Alex on the line. Instead, she pulled over, switched her phone to speaker, and began texting him frantically. She sent message after message, explaining the situation, and then instructed him to meet her at the school. Once she finished texting, she quickly resumed driving while trying to keep Alex calm.

Although her words were spoken with determination, they also evoked the same fear that Alex felt as he looked around for a place to hide. The restroom was now too far away; if he ran, the shooter might spot him. He scanned the hallway, his eyes darting to the nearest classroom, but the door was already barricaded. The students inside remained oblivious to his plight.

His mind raced, desperately searching for an escape from this nightmare. Then, out of the corner of his eye, he noticed a janitor's closet a few feet away. It was small, barely big enough to fit one person, but it might be his only chance for survival. With his heart pounding, Alex dashed towards it, praying with each step that the shooter wasn't nearby. He reached the closet and yanked the door open, slipping inside and quietly pulling it shut behind him.

Inside the closet, it was dark, with only a small beam of light filtering through the gap beneath the door. The sharp, pungent scent of cleaning supplies filled the air, but Alex didn't care. Crouched in the corner, his breath came in shallow, rapid gasps. The phone was still clutched in his hand, his mother's voice a soft murmur in his ear, reassuring him and urging him to stay strong while promising that everything would be okay. He wanted to believe her, but fear pressed down on him like a weight.

As he sat hidden away in the darkness, the reality of the situation began to sink in. He was alone, separated from his friends and teachers, with nothing but a thin door and a few feet of space between him and the shooter. The minutes dragged on, each feeling like an hour, and the silence was broken only by occasional distant shouts or the faint sound of footsteps echoing down the hall.

Alex's mind was a whirlwind of thoughts—would he survive this? Would he see his family again? Would this nightmare ever end? He tried to push the thoughts away by focusing on his mother's voice and the sound of her calm, steady breathing, but it was hard. The fear was too strong, too all-consuming. All he could do was wait, pray, and hope that help would arrive before it was too late.

As Alex cried, his mother's heart shattered. She fought to keep her emotions in check while speeding towards the school.

"I know you're scared, baby, but I am here. Just listen to my voice. I'm on my way, okay?"

Alex began to sob harder, and his mother did her best to calm him.

"Alex, you need to stay quiet. Help is coming, but you have to be very quiet, okay?"

"I'm scared, Mom," Alex whispered, his voice shaking.

"I know, baby. Did you find somewhere safe to hide?"

"I'm in the janitor's closet."

"Good, good. Can you lock the door?"

"I don't know, Mom. I don't know if it has a lock on it."

"Can you check, baby? I really need you to do that for me."

"Okay," Alex sobbed.

"First, listen. Do you hear anything?"

"No. It's quiet now. I'm so scared, Mom."

"Try to stay calm, baby. I'm here with you, and your dad is on his way from work. He's trying his best to get there as quickly as he can. Okay?"

"Yes, Mom," Alex replied softly.

"Now, listen. I want you to see if you can lock the door. Can you do that?"

"I can try."

With his legs shaking and hands trembling, Alex slowly stood up from his crouched position and tiptoed to the door.

"Mom, there's no lock," he told her.

"How about something you can put in front of the door to block it?" his mother suggested, desperately searching for ways to keep her son safe from the other end of the line.

Alex quickly scanned the small space, his eyes wide.

"I don't see anything big enough."

"Can you tie the door with something?"

"With what, Mom?"

"Anything. What are you wearing?"

Alex described the typical attire for a teenage boy:

sweatpants, a white t-shirt, sneakers, and an oversized hoodie.

"Take off your hoodie, baby, and use it to tie the door."

"What if he hears me?"

"Alex, you have to try. Now, put the phone on the floor, wrap your shirt around the door handle, and tie it tightly. Do this as quietly as you can."

After doing as instructed, he picked the phone back up.

"Okay, Mom, I tied it."

"Good job, Alex. You're so brave."

"What do I do now?"

"I want you to see if there is anywhere in there where you can hide."

"I can't, Mom. The room is small. There's nowhere to hide."

"Okay. Then dim the light all the way on your phone, and wait, baby. Don't hang up. Just wait. "

When Alex's mother arrived at the school, she was greeted with a chaotic scene. Police cars, ambulances, and news vans surrounded the area while a helicopter hovered overhead.

As Alex and his mother waited for this nightmare to end, her mind was filled with regret over the argument they had that morning. She had gone to his room to make sure he was up and getting ready for school. However, when she tried to open the door, the clothes piled on the floor in front of it made it nearly impossible. Upon entering and seeing the disarray of his room, her anger flared. Just two weeks ago, she had spent hours cleaning the room, and now it looked as if she had never set foot inside. Not only was the room filthy, but it also smelled like a musty locker room filled with sweaty athletes.

"Alex, I've asked you a hundred times to clean your room," his mother said, her patience visibly wearing thin as she stood in the doorway with her arms crossed, surveying the mess.

Clothes were strewn across the floor, empty snack wrappers cluttered his desk, and an unmade bed sat in the middle of it all like a neglected island.

Slouched on his bed with earbuds in and listening to music, Alex barely looked up from his phone as he replied, "I'll do it later, Mom. It's not even that bad."

"Not that bad?" she echoed incredulously, her eyes widening with disbelief as she stepped further into the room. "Alex, you can't even see the floor! This isn't up for debate; it needs to be done now."

He rolled his eyes, irritation evident on his face.

"Why are you always on my case? It's just a room. Who cares?"

"I care!" she shot back, her voice rising with frustration.

"You need to learn responsibility. I'm tired of repeatedly asking you to do simple things like cleaning up after yourself. It's not that hard, Alex."

"Mom, it's not that serious. You're making a big deal out of nothing."

Before she could respond, Alex stormed past her, grabbing his jacket from the chair by the door.

"You know what? I'm outta here."

That was their last interaction, and she felt devastated as she recalled it.

Suddenly, the door handle rattled violently. Alex's heart pounded in his chest as the makeshift barricade strained under the intruder's force.

"Mom, he's here," Alex choked out, his voice trembling with fear.

"Stay calm, Alex. Stay—"

Alex's scream abruptly cut her off. "He's here!"

The shooter pulled on the door, fighting to open it. When he finally succeeded, their eyes locked.

"Please...please don't," Alex whimpered, tears blurring his vision. Then, as the shooter raised his weapon, Alex cried out, "I love you, Mom."

In that moment, it felt as if time had come to a standstill. Yet, he could still hear his mother's voice—faint but full of love—in his ear.

A single shot pierced the fragile sanctuary of the

room, and as Alex collapsed, the phone slipped from his hand. His mother's frantic cries resonated through the receiver, her world crumbling in an instant.

In Classroom 103, students huddled together in silence, their hearts growing increasingly heavy with each gunshot blast that echoed through the halls.

Just as Alex collapsed, a cold rush of terror washed over him, his vision narrowing, the world spinning. But then, as if on cue, there was a thunderous noise outside the front entrance to the school. The shooter's attention snapped to the door, and in that instant, the door burst open, revealing a wave of law enforcement officers clad in full riot gear. Their presence was overwhelming, and they were prepared for the worst.

The police stormed the building with precision, their weapons drawn and their movements sharp. They had heard the multiple gunshots ringing through the halls and knew they had seconds to act.

Realizing the situation was slipping from his grasp, the shooter attempted to flee, darting past the officers and through the corridors, desperate to escape. But the officers were faster. They chased him down the hallway, their shouts commanding him to stop falling on deaf ears. The shooter's flight was short-lived, though. Within moments, he was tackled to the ground, his weapon pried from his hands, and the danger was quickly neutralized. The officers secured him, cuffing him tightly as he was dragged out of the school, his attempts to break free futile against the swarming law enforcement.

Meanwhile, Alex lay motionless on the floor, blood pooling around him from the gunshot to his chest. His breath was shallow, and every heartbeat felt like it would be his last. His world was slipping away, but still, he clung to life, though every ounce of his strength was drained.

On the other end of the line, Alex's mother's heart shattered as she heard the sound of chaos in the background. Her mind raced, imagining the worst scenarios. She had heard the gunfire and her son cry out—then silence. The phone connection was still open, but she couldn't reach him. Her wails of grief filled the schoolyard, a mother's pain so raw it could break anyone who heard it.

But then an unexpected breath. The faintest hint of a heartbeat, the smallest sign that Alex was still alive, even after everything.

The police worked quickly, clearing the building and securing the area. As they gathered the injured, they confirmed the devastating news: three students had been shot. However, in a strange twist of fate, all of them were still clinging to life, their wounds grave but not fatal. Paramedics rushed to the scene, their skilled hands moving rapidly to treat the students and stabilize them.

As paramedics wheeled Alex out on a stretcher, his mother's legs gave way beneath her, and she collapsed to her knees, tears of both relief and anguish flooding her face. For a moment, she thought she had lost him. The image of her son lying lifeless had burned into her mind, but now, seeing him alive—barely, but alive—she let out a breath she didn't realize she was holding.

"Thank you, God," she whispered, her voice trembling as she looked up at the sky, her heart overflowing with gratitude.

She gathered herself and reached out to touch her son's hand, knowing that even in the worst of times, life had a way of holding on. Her son was not dead. Not yet. There was still time, and with every second, there was hope.

The paramedics moved quickly, trying to stabilize Alex for transport. His injuries were critical, but his pulse remained steady—barely. His mother remained at his side as they rushed him to the waiting ambulance, her prayers a quiet mantra amid the chaos around them.

The students at Franklin High School lost their sense of security in a place that was once a safe haven for them. What was once a familiar and trusted environment now felt foreign and dangerous. But, by grace, no one lost their life.

Birthday Cake

by Alicia J. Evans

"Blessed are they that mourn; for they shall be comforted."

Matthew 5:4

YVONNE SLOWLY EXHALED AS a warm feeling spread through her body while standing in the middle of her custom-made kitchen—the very kitchen she had pleaded, no, persistently begged for. Jasper, her husband of five years, did not see the need for such an expansive kitchen. His use of the kitchen only extended as far as his need for the stove to prepare a bowl of oatmeal. In contrast, Yvonne envisioned all the meals she would cook, the people she would entertain, and the gatherings that would take place around the kitchen table.

Yvonne insisted that their renovated kitchen have large windows to let the early morning sunlight pour in. The sun's rays reflecting off the white walls and the checkered black-and-white backsplash was always a great way for her to greet the morning. She recalled how Jasper often complained about the lack of privacy because of the many windows. He would suggest adding curtains, but Yvonne always countered with, "What's the point of the windows if we're going to cover them up?"

Pulling her belt tighter around her thirty-six-inch waist, she was glad she had decided to slip on the terry cloth robe this morning. She had initially hated the robe—a Christmas gift from Jasper—because she felt it was a thoughtless gift. She thought he hadn't put much thought into picking out this gift. But now, she couldn't seem to live without it. Her husband had actually thought a lot about the robe when he decided to get it for her. He told her that he knew how much she loved lounging around watching movies and often complained about it being a bit chilly in the house. Yvonne chuckled at the memory, as today was no different. This February, an unseasonable chill had settled in the house.

Yvonne recalled how Jasper hated February, his birthday month. He never wanted to go anywhere. "It's too cold and dreary," he would complain.

"Today is one of those days," Yvonne murmured as she prepared her morning coffee.

Turning to look at the television mounted on the wall, she noticed that CBS weatherman Lonnie Quinn had his sleeves rolled up.

Smiling, she remembered Jasper saying, "If Lonnie's sleeves are rolled up, then we're in for a bad one." Her hand holding the warm coffee mug started to shake. With that brief memory, she was reminded that she had a lot to do today.

Last night before bed, Yvonne set two sticks of unsalted butter on the black marble counter. Over the years, she discovered that she liked to leave the butter out overnight so it could gradually reach room temperature. Additionally, she premeasured all the dry ingredients: flour, sugar, brown sugar, salt, baking powder, baking soda, cinnamon, and nutmeg, placing them in various Tupperware bowls that she left on the counter.

As she inhaled the robust aroma of her morning coffee, Yvonne flipped through her recipe notebook binder. It was organized by occasion: Anniversary Dinner, Christmas Dinner, Thanksgiving Dinner, Birthday Dinner, Holiday Cakes, Birthday Cakes, and Just Because Cakes. Although she had already planned to make Jasper's favorite, Carrot Cake, for his birthday, she browsed through the recipes just in the slight chance she felt inspired to change her mind.

In the early years of their marriage, Yvonne would order a custom-made cake from one of the Black-owned bakeries in Harlem. The cakes were perfect for Facebook and Instagram posts, but they always lacked something. It wasn't until Jasper cut up one of the cakes and made sure everyone took a slice home, leaving nothing behind, that he looked at Yvonne and requested her to bake him her famous carrot cake. He expressed how much he loved her baking and said he would have preferred one of her cakes for his birthday. Yvonne playfully punched him in the chest. Laughing, she told him he just wanted to see her in an apron covered in flour.

After finishing her coffee, Yvonne glanced at the clock. Realizing time was getting away from her, she went to the refrigerator and took out the milk and a block of cream cheese. She was grateful she had prepared ahead and shredded the four large carrots the night before, which she had stored in the fridge. She took them out and placed the bowl on the counter. Taking a moment to survey everything, she made sure she had everything needed for Jasper's birthday cake.

Slapping her forehead, she went into the pantry to get the missing ingredients: applesauce and confectioner's sugar. She then grabbed four small, round silicone Tupperware molds that had become her favorite cake pans.

"Damn!" Yvonne yelled as a canister filled with flour tipped over and landed on her foot.

With white flour now covering her robe and the floor,

she jumped up and down in agony. Yvonne collapsed to the floor and cried out solemnly in pain.

"Not today! Not today!"

Yvonne tightened her robe's belt even more to fend off the sudden breeze she felt. Reaching up, she grasped the edge of the countertop and pulled herself up from the floor. She straightened herself and instinctively patted the pockets of her robe; her phone was not there. In a state of confusion, she looked around the kitchen frantically, then remembered that she had left it plugged into the charger. The phone was still upstairs in the bedroom. Relieved, she let out an exasperated breath and pleaded with herself to pull it together.

Jasper's birthday had always been a big deal for Yvonne. She loved celebrating her husband. He wasn't big on going out, so Yvonne would organize a dinner party with family and friends. She spent weeks planning the menu. Besides entertaining and cooking, baking was Yvonne's favorite pastime. The menu always included Jasper's favorite dishes: broiled salmon, fried catfish, crabcakes, fried chicken, red rice, sautéed spinach, mac and cheese, and his mother's honey cornbread muffins. While he would enjoy the evening, his highlight would always be when Yvonne brought out the birthday cake, which he insisted she make. With a wide, cheesy grin, he would tell everyone his WIFE made his cake. He would brag all night, "Don't you wish your wife could make a cake like this?" And for good measure, he would add, "No one is getting a to-go slice." Everyone would laugh and cheer him on. Jasper was always the biggest court jester. Instead of this memory putting Yvonne in a jovial mood, it left her in a slight panic.

Again, noticing the time on the wall clock, she frantically patted her head and felt a few loose locs that had escaped her hair bonnet. She tucked them away and then pressed the preheat button on the stainless-steel stove. Yvonne closed her eyes and inhaled deeply in an attempt to calm her racing heart. Slowly opening her eyes, she glanced down at the stove and smiled, remembering how her husband had fought her tooth and nail when she asked him for the stainless-steel appliance package. She knew her gourmet kitchen needed the right appliances to set it off. Like everything else, Jasper eventually gave in, and she got her top-of-the-line stainless steel appliances.

Quickly, Yvonne washed her hands in the sink. This sink was the only thing in the kitchen that Jasper insisted on. He would tell her that while growing up, he always liked the idea of having a double sink in the kitchen. He also wanted a touchless faucet. Yvonne didn't quite understand that request, but hey, if that was all he wanted, she was happy to oblige. As she washed her hands, she smiled gratefully because the touchless faucet added a touch of elegance to the kitchen.

Gathering the recipe from her binder, Yvonne felt a sense of melancholy. It didn't matter how many times she made this cake; she still used the recipe. It was more out of habit than necessity. After mixing all the ingredients, she divided the batter into the four round pans. In the oven they went, and the timer was set for thirty minutes. Yvonne noted that she would check the cakes after twenty-five minutes as a precaution.

This was usually the time when Jasper would burst into the kitchen, laughing at the sight of flour dust on Yvonne's apron. He would lean against the counter, dip his finger into the bowl to scrape a fingertip full of the remaining batter, dab it on her lips, and then kiss it off.

After the cakes finished baking, she removed them from the oven and set them on the cooling rack. Ten minutes later, she removed each cake from its pan to allow it to cool completely. Next, she began to prepare the cream cheese frosting.

It was now time to frost Jasper's birthday cake. Yvonne frosted the first layer, then the second, continuing until every layer was covered in sweetness. As she admired the cake, she suddenly remembered she had forgotten the pecans. Jasper loved the addition of chopped pecans on the frosting rather than in the cake.

How could she forget the pecans?

She searched the pantry, certain there was at least one bag. Checking the time, she realized she had to hurry.

"Where are the pecans?" she muttered while wiping sweat from her brow with the sleeve of her robe.

Yvonne had taken the time to organize the pantry so she could find everything, but now she couldn't find the damn pecans.

As a feeling of trepidation began to consume her, she desperately asked the empty kitchen, "Where are the pecans?"

This birthday cake had to be perfect. It wouldn't be perfect without them.

Suddenly, Yvonne found it hard to breathe. She yanked open her terry cloth robe; it felt like it was choking her. She began knocking canisters to the floor, toppling baskets filled with chips and cookies in her frantic search for the pecans. Yvonne dropped to her knees as the tears pooling in her eyes threatened to spill over. She quietly prayed for the pecans to appear. She knew she needed to calm down and remember where she had last stored them. As she knelt on the floor, she looked down, and there they were: a bag of unopened pecans lying next to an unopened bag of Doritos.

Relieved, Yvonne closed her eyes and offered a quick prayer of thanks for finding the pecans. As she looked around at the mess she had made in the kitchen, she shrugged and laughed. If Jasper had walked into the kitchen right then, he would have covered his eyes, turned around, and run back out, laughing and saying, "I can't be a witness."

In the distance, Yvonne heard the "We Are Family" ringtone from upstairs, letting her know Jasper's brother was calling, but she needed to finish the cake, so she ignored it.

She was now sure she had subconsciously left her phone upstairs. Knowing what today was, she wanted all her focus to be on his birthday cake. Yvonne wished she had just as easily ignored the ringtone two years ago.

"Just The Way You Are" was her and Jasper's wedding song. She knew it had to be Jasper calling her to see if she needed anything else from the store. At the last minute, she realized there were no chopped pecans in the house. The guests were expected any minute, so Jasper went to the supermarket to pick up some chopped pecans and Doritos. Even though there were enough chips, he said Doritos were a must-have.

When their guests arrived, Jasper still hadn't returned home. Yvonne excused herself and left everyone in Jasper's brother's care while she went to call her husband to find out what was taking him so long. She also needed to get dressed since she was still in her robe and apron, both covered in flour. When she heard Bruno Mars playing on her phone, she was about to give Jasper a piece of her mind, but the voice on the other end was not her husband.

It was an officer asking if she was Mrs. Jasper Jaxon. Once she confirmed that she was, he informed her that there had been a bad car accident at an intersection. The driver of another vehicle ran a stop sign and collided with Jasper's car, causing it to flip and then be struck by a tractor-trailer on the opposite side of the road. He told her they were rushing him to the nearest hospital and that she should meet them there.

Yvonne arrived at the hospital as quickly as possible, but unfortunately, it was too late. Jasper was pronounced dead en route while in the ambulance.

With the missing pecans now found, Yvonne solemnly chopped the pecans to the fine consistency that Jasper preferred. She then decoratively added the chopped pecans to Jasper's four-layer carrot cake.

Yvonne stepped back from the finished birthday cake. Tears began to fall as she started her husband's birthday celebration.

"Happy Birthday, baby. I know you were thinking I forgot the pecans, but I promise you, beloved, I will never forget the pecans for your birthday cake ever again."

Lay Down My Life for You
by Eva Tremaine

A mother's love knows no bound;
there are no limits to what she will do to protect her child.

TRINITY'S HEART RACED AS she pounded on the door.

"Come on, Ms. Jacobs! Please be home!" she murmured urgently to herself.

She knew she had to get help fast before Trey was seriously hurt. Trinity and Trey both lived in the Baisley Projects in Southside Jamaica Queens. In this part of town, you should never be caught slipping, as the consequences could be fatal.

Trinity had taken the stairs two steps at a time to reach the fourth floor as quickly as she could. Despite the loud banging, Ms. Jacobs didn't answer, but Trinity kept knocking because she was certain she had to be home. Trinity spent a lot of time with Trey, Ms. Jacobs' son, so she was always at his house and knew his mother's schedule like the back of her hand. It was after 5:30 p.m., and Ms. Jacobs would likely be in the kitchen throwing down.

Just as Trinity was about to give up, she heard the bolt slide back. Ms. Jacobs swung the door open, ready to curse out whoever was on the other side. However, upon seeing the frantic look on Trinity's face, her irritation was immediately replaced with concern.

"Ms. Jacobs, they're after Trey! They're jumping him downstairs," Trinity blurted, her words tumbling over each other.

Ms. Jacobs' eyes widened briefly before she sprang into action.

"Get my phone from the kitchen counter and grab my bag from the bedroom," she instructed swiftly, her voice calm despite the urgency.

She swiftly switched her slippers for sneakers while Trinity complied without hesitation, knowing every second counted. Trinity snatched up the phone and Ms. Jacobs' bag, which held everything from band-aids to cash for emergencies. Unbeknownst to Trinity, it also concealed a stun gun.

As they hurried to the door, Trinity heard Ms. Jacobs mutter a quick prayer under her breath. With the elevator out of service once again, they rushed down the stairs,

Ms. Jacobs gripping Trinity's hand tightly along the way. The sounds of commotion and shouting grew louder as they neared the ground floor. Trinity dashed out of the building with Ms. Jacobs close behind, hurrying to get to Trey.

"What happened?" Ms. Jacobs asked Trinity as they rushed toward the sounds of a rowdy crowd.

"Trey got into it with Leroy, and Leroy's friend Devon jumped in."

"Where's Eli?" Ms. Jacobs questioned.

"I have no idea. I was wondering the same thing."

The last time Trinity tried to intervene in a disagreement between Trey and some other boys, he had refused to speak to her for weeks. He argued that her interference made him seem weak. She had searched for Eli, Trey's best friend, but he was nowhere to be found. Normally inseparable, Eli was absent when Trey needed him the most. Trey's adversaries seized the opportunity when he was vulnerable, leaving Trinity feeling desperate to help him. Compelled to take action and unwilling to stand by while others attacked her man, she rushed to get his mother.

As they turned the corner, the fight came into view. Quickly handing Trinity her bag, Ms. Jacobs stepped forward, her authoritative presence felt immediately. She had no qualms about pushing through the crowd to get to Trey, who was pinned against the wall but holding his own against the boys attacking him. This wasn't the first time he had faced these two. Known for his fighting skills inherited from his father, Trey was a formidable opponent on his own. Despite being outnumbered, he fought fiercely to defend himself.

Just as Trinity and Ms. Jacobs approached, Trey was thrown to the ground and viciously kicked in the face. In their neighborhood, bystanders were quick to gather and watch but were reluctant to intervene. Getting involved in such altercations was risky, and while some may have wanted to help by stepping in, most simply stood by and observed the violence unfold.

Ms. Jacobs was far from an ordinary mother; she was a force of nature and a protector who wouldn't hesitate to confront anyone, even if they were just children. Her maternal instincts were sharp and her sense of justice unwavering. So, when she saw her child being mercilessly kicked while on the ground, something inside her snapped. In that moment, she became a whirlwind of fury, charging at the group of boys with the speed and intensity of a mother bear protecting her cub. Her fists flew with the ferocity of someone who had grown up scrapping alongside her brothers, learning to stand her ground in a world that didn't always play fair.

With each blow she delivered, her movements were

fueled by a primal determination to protect her child. Her fists struck with relentless rhythm, each impact sending a message that echoed her fierce resolve. In the midst of the flurry of punches, she shouted with a voice that was both commanding and desperate.

"Leave Trey alone! Get away from him!"

Her words, brimming with anger and urgency, sliced through the chaos like a blade.

Caught off guard by the sudden onslaught, the boys initially mistook the figure charging at them for Eli. They spun around, ready to retaliate, only to encounter a fierce and unexpected force. Ms. Jacobs' relentless blows landed with the precision and power of a skilled fighter. The boys, who prided themselves on being tough, suddenly found themselves on the receiving end of a fury they had never anticipated. Each blow left them increasingly disoriented and stunned, their bravado rapidly dissolving under her unwavering assault.

Despite their rough exterior, the boys had enough street smarts to know when they were outmatched. Their confidence faltered as they realized this was no ordinary adult; Ms. Jacobs was a force to be reckoned with, and they were no longer in control of the situation. One by one, they began to back away, distancing themselves from Trey, who had scrambled to his feet, ready for another round. His adrenaline surged, and his eyes darted between his mother, Leroy, and Devon—unsure of what would happen next.

The ringleader, Leroy, sneered at Trey with a contemptuous glare.

"You got your mama fighting for you now?" he spat.

His voice was laced with mockery, but there was an edge of uncertainty in his tone as if he couldn't quite believe they had been bested by someone's mother. Leroy's bravado was all that he had left to cling to, even as he inwardly recognized he had lost this battle.

Trey was furious that his mother had intervened to help him in his fight, but his main focus now was on getting back at Leroy for humiliating him. He glanced knowingly at Trinity, silently acknowledging her role in bringing his mother into the fray. She returned his look innocently, feigning ignorance of the situation. He understood her intentions were good, but she needed to learn to stay out of men's affairs. He resolved to address this with her later. For now, his mind was set on one thing: settling the score.

Without any hesitation, Trey leaned back and struck Leroy, sending him flying back and crashing to the ground. Before he could react, Trey was on top of him, fists raining down on his face with unrelenting fury. Blood splattered, and Leroy's eyes widened in shock and pain.

Devon stood frozen, watching helplessly. He knew he couldn't jump in; Trey was making an example out of Leroy, and any interference would only escalate things. Ms. Jacobs stood nearby, her expression stern and unforgiving. She didn't attempt to break up the fight. In her eyes, the punk deserved every bit of the beating her son was delivering. Maybe next time, he'd think twice about jumping Trey. Trinity stood a few feet away, her eyes fixed on Trey. A sense of pride swelled within her as she watched him defend himself. This was her man, and she admired his strength and determination.

Once Ms. Jacobs sensed that Leroy had learned his lesson, she gently tugged on Trey's arm, signaling that it was time to walk away. She could feel the tension still radiating from him, but her touch was firm and reassuring, letting him know they had made their point. Trey hesitated for a moment, his adrenaline still pumping, but eventually, he nodded in reluctant agreement. He knew he had given Leroy a thorough beating, and deep down, he felt that justice had been served.

As Trey stepped back, the energy around them shifted. The crowd that had gathered to witness the fight began to lose interest, slowly dispersing in search of their next source of excitement. The thrill of the spectacle was fading, and the onlookers, sensing that the show was over, drifted away in groups, murmuring among themselves about what they had just witnessed.

Leroy slowly pushed himself up from the ground, wincing as he assessed his injuries. His face burned with a mixture of embarrassment and lingering pain as he brushed off the dirt, trying to regain his composure. However, the damage was done; he had been humiliated, and there was no denying it. Devon stood beside him, casting dark, angry glances at Trey and his mother. The anger in his eyes was evident, yet there was also a wariness, a recognition that Ms. Jacobs and Trey were not to be underestimated.

Standing tall beside his mother, Trey stared back at them with a steely resolve. His gaze was unflinching, daring them to make a move, to try anything further. He was ready, fists still clenched, heart still racing from the adrenaline of victory. Yes, Trey had handled Leroy, but he was far from finished. Trey made a mental note that Devon, who had also attacked him, still had his reckoning coming. His eyes narrowed slightly as he thought of the payback that awaited Devon, the satisfaction of knowing that he would make sure no one messed with him again. They would all learn that he wasn't someone to be played with—not now, not ever.

Leroy and Devon retreated, with Leroy nursing his bruised ego and plotting his revenge.

As they headed back to the building, Trinity praised Trey for getting back at Leroy and giving him a good beating. In response, Trey expressed that he didn't appreciate her bringing his mother into the situation.

"What else was I supposed to do? They were hurting you, and I couldn't find Eli."

"Eli went to visit his dad, but that's still no excuse. My mom? Really?"

"Trey, leave Trinity alone," Ms. Jacobs intervened. "It's not her fault. She was just trying to help. And thank God she did come get me. I can't imagine what would have happened if I hadn't shown up."

"I would've been fine, Mom. This isn't the first time they've jumped me, and it might not be the last. I told you not to worry. I can handle myself in these streets," Trey boasted.

Caught up in their conversation, Trey, Trinity, and Ms. Jacobs were oblivious to the danger lurking nearby. Leroy, seething with rage and humiliation, watched them from a distance, his grip tightening around the baseball bat he held. The memory of Trey besting him still burned in his mind, an insult he could never let stand. He couldn't admit it, not even to himself, but he knew deep down that he and Devon were no match for Trey. That truth festered inside him, twisting his anger into something darker and more dangerous.

Determined to reclaim his pride and teach Trey a lesson he would never forget, Leroy leaned in close to Devon, whispering a few quick words. With a silent nod, the two began to move, their steps deliberate and menacing. The bat felt solid in Leroy's hands, a tool of revenge that promised to even the score. As they closed in on their target, their eyes locked on Trey, intent on making him pay.

Out of the corner of her eye, Ms. Jacobs saw Leroy rapidly approaching. The sudden movement triggered her instincts, and in an instant, she realized what was about to happen. Her thoughts shot to her bag, but there was not enough time. Her heart pounded in her chest, the adrenaline surge quick and intense as her body reacted before her mind could fully process the threat. She had only moments to act, but that was all she needed.

Without a second thought, Ms. Jacobs threw herself in front of Trey, using her body as a shield to absorb the incoming blow. Everything seemed to go in slow motion as Leroy's bat swung through the air with a chilling whoosh, its deadly arc aimed directly at her son. The force of the impact was brutal, and the bat made a metallic thud as it struck her skull. The sound echoed through the neighborhood, a grim punctuation to the violence that had erupted.

Ms. Jacobs' body went limp instantly, collapsing to

the ground, her eyes wide with shock and pain. The world seemed to tilt as Trey and Trinity's screams pierced the air, raw and filled with terror. They rushed to her side, their hearts hammering in their chests as they took in the horrific sight of her lifeless form sprawled on the grass. The bat, now stained with blood, rolled to a stop nearby, a silent witness to the brutal attack. Leroy and Devon immediately fled, leaving chaos in their wake.

As Trey watched his mother drop to the ground, it felt as though time itself had fractured, shattering into a million jagged pieces that sliced through his very soul. A tidal wave of shock, disbelief, and horror crashed over him, drowning him in emotions too immense to process. His heart seemed to stop, suspended in a moment of unbearable grief, while the world around him faded into a muted, dreamlike silence. Everything slowed, blurring as the gravity of the situation began to sink in.

Guilt gnawed at him, its sharp claws digging deep into his chest. She had endured the blow intended for him, and that realization felt like a vice tightening around his heart, crushing him under its heaviness. If only he had seen Leroy coming. If only he had been reacted faster. If only he could have done something—anything—to prevent this. The haunting "what-ifs" swirled in his mind, intensifying the pain and despair that loomed over him.

Fear and panic surged through his veins, each pulse a desperate plea for some kind of miracle. His mind raced with fragmented prayers—frantic thoughts that somehow, someway, she would be okay. But as he stared at her motionless body, an unyielding dread took hold. A deep, gnawing terror gripped him, squeezing the air from his lungs as he grappled with the horrifying possibility that he might never hear her voice again, feel the warmth of her embrace, or see her loving smile.

The image of her lying there, motionless, with her eyes closed and colorless face, etched itself into his mind with a searing intensity that left him paralyzed. It was an image he knew he would carry with him for the rest of his life, a haunting reminder of the sacrifice she had made. The finality of the moment—the unspoken goodbye, the love she had shown in her last, desperate act—crushed him beneath the weight of grief he couldn't yet fully comprehend.

Trey dropped to his knees beside her, the impact jolting him back into the chaotic present. Around him, the scene erupted into total turmoil—shouts, gasps, and the distant wail of sirens blending into a symphony of noise. Yet, everything felt distant, a mere echo compared to the deafening silence in his mind. He grasped his mother's hand, desperate for her touch, and felt the world he knew crumble into pieces around him. In that moment, Trey realized the depth of his mother's love—a love so fierce and unyielding that she had made the heart-wrenching choice to lay down her life to protect him.

A Sister's Love
by Alicia J. Evans

"Let all that you do be done in love."

1 Corinthians 16:14

WHAT WAS SHE THINKING coming back home after all this time? Five years ago, she had escaped the madness of her life, promising herself she would never return.

"Miss, this is it," the Uber driver says, looking at her through his rearview mirror.

She meets his gaze and notices the impatience in his look. *How long has he been parked here?* she wonders. Then she hears the ping of his phone, signaling that he had another pickup.

"I'm sorry, I've changed my mind. Can you take me back to the airport?"

With his eyebrows furrowed and lips pressed together, he stares at her for a moment before responding, "Sure, but I will need to charge you for the new trip."

Madison Bentley stares out the window as her childhood home begins to fade from view. Once upon a time, she would have been full of joy at the sight of it. She grew up in the home with her parents, her older brother Damon, and her older sister Danielle. Madison was the youngest of the three, and because of the fourteen-year age difference between her and Danielle, she was often referred to as the surprise baby.

Thinking back, she can recall Damon and his friends playing a quick game of one-on-one in their yard while Danielle and her girlfriends cheered from the sidelines for the cutest boy to win. Back then, the boys didn't care that the basketball hoop nailed to the garage was missing its net or that the driveway was cracked and uneven. All they knew was that house number 106-15 was the place to be all summer long. Madison, however, was never allowed to join them because she was much younger; they said she cramped their style. She would watch them from the kitchen window, and Damon would give her a thumbs-up every time he made a shot. The memory of her brother Damon warmed Madison's heart.

Once the house is out of view, Madison throws her head back and closes her eyes. She isn't ready to face anyone just yet, especially Danielle.

Growing up, Madison wanted to be like Danielle. Even though she was much younger than Danielle, she followed her sister everywhere. Madison even received her hand-me-downs, which she wore with pride. As a child, Madison found joy in sneaking into Danielle's room and slipping her small feet into her sister's shoes. Of course, they were too big, but that didn't matter to Madison. Danielle was her hero.

That was so long ago, Madison thinks, sighing wearily.

She knows they will get caught in the evening rush hour traffic on their way back to the airport at this time of day. So, in an effort to feel a bit more comfortable, she kicks off her three-inch Jimmy Choos and sinks deeper into the leather seat. She lets out a heavy breath of instant relief.

When Madison left home, she was twenty years old and in her second year at Hofstra University. Size eighteen, fashionable leggings were her must-have attire, and she always sported a pair of athletic sneakers or Crocs. She never felt the need to wear makeup; a little MAC natural lip gloss was the most she would dare to apply. If she felt adventurous, she would add a tint of color to the lip gloss.

Why do I feel like I need to be dressed to the tee, even to the point of wearing heels, to see my family?

She asks herself this question, even though she knows the answer. She wants to show them that she is doing fine without them.

While sitting in traffic on the Grand Central Parkway, Madison digs into her Dooney & Bourke bag and pulls out her cosmetic case. She fishes around for her compact mirror to apply a coat of her MAC Ruby Roo lipstick, even though she doesn't really need it. Then, she tilts the mirror and checks her hair for any out-of-place strands. Of course, there are none. There was a time when she couldn't care less about her hair.

"Sit still, Maddie. You're going to make me burn you."

"Mama, I don't want curls. I like when you braid my hair."

"Maddie, it's picture day. You're getting curls. Now sit still."

She sheds a tear as she remembers that day as if it were yesterday.

Madison knows she should have gone into the house; she is sure they are all there waiting for her. After Damon informed her that Danielle was diagnosed with Stage 4 lung cancer and that the doctors said there was nothing they could do for her, he told her over the phone, "She has been asking for you." She contemplated for two days before deciding to purchase her airline ticket. She realized that returning home was not going to be easy. All her hard work and determination to put the past behind her went out the window the moment she asked the driver to take her back to the airport.

After handing the driver a fifty-dollar bill, she walks

over to stand in line for the shuttle to the hotel. She glances back at her driver and sees him still standing there in shock at the size of the tip. Madison knows that she had already arranged for a tip to be included when her credit card was charged for the trip, but she appreciated the driver for not putting her out of his car and making her request a new ride. She also didn't forget the fact that he turned down another fare. So, giving him something extra was her way of saying thank you. When the driver looks up, their eyes meet, and she flashes him a sincere smile. Madison lets that good feeling of making someone happy linger for a moment while she waits for the shuttle.

After a brief wait for the shuttle, she is taken to the Hilton Hotel near the airport. Once she settles into her room, she calls Damon to let him know she has arrived in town and will be over in the morning. He offers to pick her up from the airport, but she tells him that she has already checked into her hotel. Madison can hear the disappointment in his voice. Of all her family members, Damon is the one she hates to disappoint.

After they hang up, Madison decides to go down to the bar located in the lobby. A few people are seated at the tables, and even fewer are at the bar. She chooses to sit there, not wanting to feel the stares for dining alone.

Madison orders a chocolate martini but then realizes

she hasn't eaten anything all day. Scanning the dinner menu, she places her order for salmon and grilled shrimp with a baked potato. She then reaches for the bowl of salted nuts on the counter, knowing better than to drink on an empty stomach. The bartender sets the drink in front of her and informs her that her meal will be ready shortly. When she looks up to thank him, she's momentarily caught off guard. Her initial reaction upon seeing this specimen of a man is, *Why is this gorgeous guy working as a bartender and not gracing the cover of a magazine?* She manages to swallow despite the lump in her throat and nods slowly, hoping he understands that her non-verbal gesture conveys thanks. As she takes a sip of her martini, she can't help but think he must rake in a lot of tips looking that fine. The sleeves of his t-shirt, which bears the bar's name, Lenny's, across the front, stretch tightly across his biceps.

"Damn," Madison mutters and then looks around to make sure no one heard her.

She peeks over the bar at the bartender while he busies himself pouring drinks.

It should be illegal for one man to look that damn good, Madison thinks as she fans herself with a napkin, fantasizing about all the things she would do to him if the opportunity presented itself.

As she waits for her dinner, she learns that the

bartender's name is Mike. He's not just the bartender; he owns the bar.

"If you're the owner, why the name Lenny's?" Madison asks, pointing at his shirt.

He explains that the bar is named after his Cane Corso, Leonardo. Hence, the logo of a dog's face. Turning her head to look around, she notices the emblem displayed throughout the space.

"Got it," she says with a laugh.

She mentions that she is originally from New York but moved to Atlanta five years ago. Madison does not understand why she is chatting so freely with this stranger.

Maybe what they say about bartenders being easier to talk to and cheaper than a psychiatrist is true, she thinks to herself.

They continue talking until her meal finally arrives.

As she put the last piece of salmon in her mouth, she let out a satisfying sigh and whispers to herself, "Dang, that was good," while dabbing the corners of her mouth with a napkin.

"You must've been famished," Mike comments as he approaches her and reaches to remove the now-empty plate while trying to stifle his laugh.

"Blame the chef for why there isn't a morsel left on that plate," Madison says, trying to explain.

"Would you like another?" he inquires, nodding towards her empty glass as he wipes down the bar where her plate and drink once sat.

Glancing at her watch and noticing it's nearly nine o'clock, she politely declines.

"No, thank you. I didn't realize it was this late."

For the first time, she hears all the chatter around her. She laughs and thinks, *Where did all these people come from?* Shrugging her shoulders, she asks Mike for the check.

"You sure I can't convince you to have another?" Mike asks, already pouring the vodka into the shaker. "This one will be on the house. Plus, the live band is about to start playing, and they're good," he adds.

"Oh, what the hell. One more drink won't hurt, and especially if it's on you and not me," Madison replies with a laugh.

* * *

When Madison enters her room, she hears the buzz of her phone notifying her that she has a voice message. She had intentionally left her phone in the room while she went downstairs to the bar. Then her phone pings, and she rolls her eyes in frustration, realizing that whoever called had sent her a text message.

"Not now! Not freaking now," she screams in the empty room as she grabs one of the liquor bottles from the small refrigerator.

Madison walks into the spacious bathroom and lets out a sigh of relief upon seeing the oversized sunken tub.

Sometimes you have to splurge on yourself, she thinks to herself while pouring the complimentary bubble bath into the tub.

Once she finishes soaking, she climbs into the king-size bed and finally takes the time to respond to some of the texts. One message she deletes without even reading it. Her family drama is overwhelming, and she can only deal with one thing at a time. Five years have not eased the pain or erased the hurt. Her choice to move away and make a life far away from her family was the best decision she ever made. Her family took keeping a secret to another level.

Madison had a passion for numbers and was destined to follow in her dad's footsteps by becoming an accountant. She maintained a 4.0 GPA during her two years at Hofstra. She always felt the need to prove that she was as smart as Danielle. To their parents' dismay, Danielle married her high school sweetheart instead of going to work with their father after college. They had been grooming Danielle all her life to take over the family accounting firm, but Danielle was happy being a wife and stay-at-home mother. Thus, her parents' focus shifted to Madison taking over the family business since Damon's life revolved solely around sports. Madison is certain her life would have been good had she stayed, but she didn't want to live with a lie staring her in the face.

Madison tosses and turns all night. She kicks the covers off and then pulls them back on. Unable to sleep, Madison gets out of bed and paces around the room for what feels like hours. Happy that the refrigerator has mini bottles of Moscato, she removes one and decides to sit in the large easy chair instead of climbing back into bed. The chair swivels, allowing Madison to turn and position herself to gaze at the New York City skyline. She is glad she picked a room on a higher floor; the view allows her to get lost in her thoughts as she takes in the beauty of her hometown.

As Madison takes a sip of the Moscato, she reflects back to that day many years ago.

Everyone was excited to attend the Bentley Family Reunion in Sumter, South Carolina. Her parents decided to make it a real family reunion by doing a road trip, wanting the whole family to travel together, and everyone had agreed. Damon was driving with his wife and kids, while Madison rode with Danielle, who had recently divorced her husband. Madison thought it would be a good time for her to spend time with her big sister and niece, Dylan. Twelve hours in a car with a five-year-old turned out to be an experience for sure. The time spent with Danielle was priceless, and their fourteen-year age difference didn't stop them from sharing stories. Madison even confided in her about the boyfriend she had been keeping a secret.

"Girl, between class and church, Daddy keeps me on lockdown," she told her sister as they laughed together about their overprotective father.

"Can you talk to him or something?" Madison begged her.

"I don't know what I can tell him. I think they were easy on me and Damon, and now they are trying not to make the same mistake with you," Danielle replied. After a brief pause, she added, "You know, when Damon and I left for school, it just left you at home with them. And with me deciding to marry Charles instead of working with Daddy, I think maybe they just want to hold on to you a little longer."

Disregarding her sister's words, Madison quickly replied, "Whatever" and sucked her teeth.

Once everyone had arrived at the hotel and freshened up, they headed to the family meet-and-greet. People were mingling and introducing themselves to each other. Madison sat at a table with a woman who introduced herself as Aunt Bertha. Madison hugged her and mentioned that she was Derrick and Mona's youngest.

"Baby, I know who you are. You look just like your momma," Aunt Bertha beamed. "Shoot, I used to keep your

momma when she came south for the summer."

Madison smiled, realizing that the old woman didn't know who she was at all. Looking at Aunt Bertha, Madison didn't believe the woman was that old to have taken care of her mother when she was younger. Laughing at the obvious confusion, Madison just shrugged while feeling a little sorry for Aunt Bertha. Madison politely made her escape by asking Aunt Bertha if she would like something to drink.

As she looked around the room, she realized her dad's side of the family was large. She wondered why they had never attended earlier family reunions and made a mental note to ask her parents when she had a moment. She had no recollection of visiting her father's family. Both of his parents had passed away before Madison was born, but she had heard talk of Aunt Bertha since she was his mother's only surviving sister. Aunt Darlene, her father's sister, and her family would visit often. Outside of them, Madison couldn't remember meeting any other cousins. She looked across the room at Aunt Bertha and wondered why she had no memory of visiting her, but clearly, Aunt Bertha knew who she was.

The light from the sun peeking through the blinds reminds her that she hasn't gotten any sleep and needs coffee. Now showered, dressed, and fueled up with the complimentary in-room coffee, she feels half-human and ready to take on the day. A lesson she learned long ago is that a fresh coat of makeup and a hot cup of coffee will have you feeling like a million bucks. Looking at the clock on the nightstand, she concedes that it's time to face the music. In the Uber heading over to the house, she braces herself for what's to come.

"Good morning. I'm on my way. I should be there in about twenty," Madison says and then disconnects the call before the conversation can go any further.

Family reunions are meant to bring families together. You get to meet relatives you may have never seen before and build new lifelong connections. Madison thought back to the moment when her family was broken, relationships shattered.

As they sat at their family table, Madison was occupied with Dylan, who had spilled juice on her dress. She noticed Aunt Bertha heading their way.

"Derrick, baby, is that you? I know that's you. Give Aunt Bertha a hug."

"Hey, Aunt Bertha, how are you? You remember my wife, Mona?"

"Yes. How you, baby?" Aunt Bertha said, pulling Mona in for a hug. "I met that grandbaby; she looks just like my Danni. Why you keeping her from her Aunt Bertha, baby? Where's my Danni?" Aunt Bertha asked as she let go of Mona and looked around for Danielle.

"Here I am, Aunt Bertha," Danielle said as Aunt Bertha quickly pulled her into a tight embrace.

Madison, having finished cleaning up Dylan, sensed a shift in the atmosphere. Her mother's face was tense, and her eyes were wide, blinking rapidly. She turned, looking at her husband in panic, pulled him over to her, and whispered something in his ear. Before he could say anything, Aunt Bertha spotted Madison sitting at the table.

While still holding onto Danielle, Aunt Bertha's eyes stayed on Madison.

"I told your daddy when you got pregnant to let you come stay with me, but he said he and your mama would take care of everything. Aunt Bertha would've loved to fatten up that baby. You know she would've loved my biscuits and gravy. Shoot, she looks just like you. I woulda known her anywhere."

"Auntie," Damon yelled as he rushed to the table with Glinda and their kids in tow.

Someone sitting at another table might have missed the shaking of Mona's head and the beads of sweat pouring down Derrick's face, but Madison caught it all. She felt as if her body were in quicksand, sinking fast. Madison slowly realized she was watching her life unfold, as if she were a character in a Saturday night Lifetime special. She searched from left to right, seeing the same look of anguish on her parents' and siblings' faces. Her mother cried silently, while her father turned to walk Aunt Bertha back to her table. Danielle dropped into her chair as if she were a rock thrown off a cliff. Damon asked Glinda to take the kids to the room. Madison, unable to breathe, looked from her mother to her sister before turning and running out of the room just as the deejay started playing "Family Reunion".

Walking through the door of her parents' home feels like stepping into a segment of *The Twilight Zone*. Nothing has changed over the years. The house is buzzing with family members. Some she has kept up with thanks to Facebook and Instagram. Others she doesn't recognize at all. Madison greets a few as she makes her way to the kitchen, where she finds her mother sitting in the corner, gazing out the window and nursing a cup of tea.

"Mama," Madison whispers as she approaches her mother.

Mona turns around upon hearing Madison's voice.

She embraces Madison in a tight hug and whispers in her ear, "I have missed you, my darling daughter."

Hearing her mother call her daughter, Madison can't hold back the tears. Being in her mother's arms allows Madison to cry like never before. She hadn't realized how much she missed her mother until that very moment.

The other people in the kitchen notice that the mother and daughter need some time alone, so they quietly step out. Mona guides Madison to a chair so they can sit down and share some time together talking.

Derrick and Damon walk into the kitchen after a

relative tells them that Madison is home. After a series of hugs and tears, the family decides it's time for all the guests to leave. With the family now alone, Derrick is the first to speak.

"Madison, I'm so happy you came home. You left before you got the full story."

Madison glances at her brother and parents. She knows she was wrong for leaving the way she did. Her parents have aged so much over the last five years. She has only kept in regular contact with Damon. Whenever her parents called her, she always had an excuse ready for why she couldn't talk. She was either in a meeting or heading into one, never taking the time to hear them out. Now, looking at them, she can see the wrinkles on their faces and the worry lines across their foreheads. The few gray strands have turned into a full head of silver hair for both. Madison has missed so much that she can only pray she has time to make it up to them.

"I'm sorry," is all Madison can muster before the tears begin to fall again.

Damon, who is watching everything unfold, understands that there is much that needs to be said. He is the only one Madison has had contact within the past five years. She made him promise not to share her whereabouts with anyone. He did not like keeping this information from his family, but he could relate to

Madison's feeling of betrayal since they had also kept the secret from him. Growing up, he can remember when Danielle and their mother went away to stay with Granny and returned with baby Madison. He only found out about the family secret when Danielle was pregnant with Dylan. Danielle has always shown strength and grace, so Damon was caught off guard when his sister showed up at his house distraught. She shared her fears about being a mother and then made him an accomplice in their family secret.

Damon shakes his head at the memory, wanting to stay in the present.

"We need to let Madison go see Danielle. This is the time for Danielle to tell Madison her story," Damon says, then pulls Madison in for an embrace and whispers in her ear, "You know you will always be my sister."

Once again, Madison is overcome with tears.

* * *

Unsure of what to expect and only relying on the bits and pieces Damon had shared with her, Madison takes a deep breath. As she exhales, she walks through the door. Frozen, she stares at the figure lying in the bed, afraid to move closer for a better look. It couldn't be Danielle. The person's frame is small, almost childlike. As she approaches, Danielle opens her eyes. Madison gasps audibly as she gazes into Danielle's eyes.

How is it that I never saw the resemblance of our eyes? It's like I'm looking into my own eyes, Madison thinks to herself.

"You came," Danielle strains to say. Her face lights up as she extends her hand toward Madison. "I didn't think you were going to come. Madison, I am so sorry. I was young and thought I was doing the best thing for you."

A lonely tear rolls down Danielle's face. With a weak voice, she tells Madison to sit next to her so she can explain.

"Can you please give me some water?" she asks, barely above a whisper. "I am tired, Maddie. But before I rest, I must tell you why."

As Madison wipes the sweat from Danielle's forehead, she says, "That can wait. You don't have to explain anything right now."

Madison sits in the chair, wringing her fingers. Her stomach starts to cramp. She looks down at Danielle, and the realization that this might be the last time she gets to talk with her mother hits her.

"My mother," she murmurs.

This is the first time she has thought of her as her mother. Madison notices Danielle's breathing is shallow. She lays her head on Danielle's stomach and cries.

"I'm sorry. I should have never run away the way I did."

"Shhh, baby. You have nothing to be sorry for," Danielle whispers as the tears fall.

"Auntie!" screams Dylan as she bursts into the room and jumps onto the bed.

Damon, fast on her heels, apologizes as he grabs her to take her out of the room.

Madison is quickly caught off guard by Dylan's appearance. For the past few years, she had kept up with Dylan through Facetime chats with Damon, but seeing her in person is kind of surreal. Dylan looks exactly like Madison did at that age. They both share the same big dark eyes and long, thick hair. While growing up, Danielle always kept her hair straight with a relaxer. Now that she wears it naturally, the resemblance is noticeable.

"No, I must tell you everything now. We don't know how much time I have," Danielle says, doing her best to sound strong.

However, Madison can hear how straining it is for her to talk. If she needs a reminder that her stubbornness has led to her losing valuable time with her family, just looking down at her fragile sister/mother is enough. Again, she begins to cry.

Danielle takes a deep breath and starts to unravel the web of lies that was Madison's life.

"I had just started high school and thought I was all

that when the captain of the basketball team showed interest in me. I gave him my virginity, and then he dumped me. I had made up my mind to get rid of it, I mean you," Danielle quickly says, correcting herself. "Mommy and Daddy were against the idea of an abortion, but they didn't want my life to end before it got started."

When Danielle stops talking, Madison thinks she has fallen asleep, but just as she stands up to leave, Danielle motions for her to sit back down.

"The medication has me going in and out," she says.

Madison tries to ensure her that she will be there when she wakes up and encourages her to go ahead and take a nap. She can only imagine how much pain Danielle must be in.

Danielle shakes her head slowly, rejecting Madison's suggestion of a nap.

"I was scared, Maddie. I did not know how I was going to take care of a baby. I loved being on the cheerleading squad and doing fun things. I was just a kid," Danielle explains as she sobs uncontrollably.

Madison gets up and walks to the other side of the room. A chill runs through her body. She shivers, wraps her arms around herself, and moves them up and down her arm, creating some warmth.

Wow! She was going to get rid of me. I was never wanted,

Madison thinks.

As she stares out the window, she recalls a time when the view was so different. The doors of all the houses would be open, with kids running in and out all day. Today, however, as she looks at the same houses, they appear dark and lonely.

Danielle lets out a low cough, and Madison rushes to her side.

Just then, the door creaks open, and her mother pokes her head into the room.

"May I come in, honey?" her mother asks.

As Madison glances at her sister and then at her mother, she starts to feel overwhelmed by the many emotions she is experiencing. Before she realizes it, she finds herself falling into her mother's arms and begins to bawl.

When the hospice nurse enters the room and tells them that she will sit with Danielle while she rests, Madison, her mother, and a few other family members head to the kitchen. After having a light lunch, all the children are taken away to give the adults some time to talk. Her father is the first to speak.

"I sure missed you, baby girl. You look good. You alright?" he asks, pulling Madison into a tight hug.

"I missed you, too," Madison hesitates. Looking into her father's eyes and seeing the hurt, she adds, "*Daddy*, I missed you, too."

With that, Madison puts her head on her father's shoulder and weeps. She weeps for the years she missed with her parents. She weeps for the time she lost with her niece, Dylan, who is actually her little sister. She weeps for her big sister, Danielle, who gave her the best gift she could ever ask for: life. She weeps because she will not have the chance to show Danielle the beautiful, successful woman she has become. She weeps because she will never get the opportunity to express her thanks. She weeps for her mother, as it was her selfless act that allowed her to grow up with two loving parents, a sister, and a brother who love and adore her.

When she finally raises her head, she looks around the room, and in that moment, she understands what love is. Secrets can tear down and break families apart. One may never understand the toll that keeping secrets takes on the secret keeper or the person from whom the truth was withheld. But it is love that will rebuild a family and make it stronger than ever.

Three Months Later...

"Yes, she is all settled in."

"Fine. I will have her call you after lunch."

Disconnecting the call, Madison laughs to herself as she thinks about her big brother, who can't stop worrying about her. It has been three months since they buried Danielle, and she finally has Dylan home with her.

After the funeral, Madison was surprised that the extended family wasn't as shocked as she expected them to be seeing her name in the obituary as Danielle's daughter. Her mother explained that after the family reunion, pieces of information had been leaking out, and if she had been around, she would have known that. Also, they all found out that all those years they thought they were keeping a secret from the family, they were actually the subject of family gossip.

Madison could not believe that Danielle had written in her will for Madison to gain custody of Dylan, with the approval of Dylan's father, who would remain actively involved in Dylan's life. He was well aware that the Bentley family played a significant role in his daughter's life and did not wish to disrupt that. With Madison living in Atlanta, the family agreed it was time for a change. Damon and his family relocated to Charleston, South Carolina, while their parents retired and moved to Decatur, Georgia. This way, everyone was in close proximity to one another.

Madison is fully aware that her life will change now that Dylan will be staying with her, but she doesn't mind. Her main focus is on making sure Dylan is taken care of.

When Madison returned home to New York, her life

in Atlanta took a hit. She had to face the reality that her unfinished family drama was affecting her life. She acted as if everything was okay, but it was not. She was settling into a relationship that took more from her than it gave. Madison understood that her role as Dylan's big sister meant she had to show up like never before.

Cutting Dylan's ham and cheese sandwich into quarters, Madison still cannot believe the similarities she, Dylan, and their mother share. Even when she was very young, Dylan only ate ham and cheese, and it had to be cut into quarters. To this day, Madison still eats her sandwiches this way.

"Dylan, lunch is ready! Dylan?"

Not getting a response, Madison hurries up the stairs to look for Dylan. When she gets to the top of the stairs, she sees the reflection from her bedroom mirror. Dylan is attempting to walk in a pair of Madison's shoes. She tries to stand but falls down instantly. After the third attempt and just when Madison decides to walk in the room, Dylan does it. She prances in front of the wardrobe mirror and admires her look. Madison quietly backs out of the room and down the stairs while silently sending up a prayer to her mother to let her know...

"We're going to be alright."

Guided By Love

by Eva Tremaine & Alicia J. Evans

NATHANIEL SAT IN HIS bedroom, surrounded by the chaos that now defined his life—so far removed from the order he once knew. He had ventured down a dark path, lost in a haze of drugs and alcohol. The room mirrored his descent: clothes were scattered across the floor, takeout containers piled high on the nightstand, and empty liquor bottles littered around. The air was thick and stale, heavy with the scent of alcohol and dirty sheets. He had been avoiding his mother, knowing full well he couldn't hide the mess he'd become. It had started innocently enough, just trying a little here and there, but soon he was addicted, chasing the rush of that first high.

Meth had become his poison of choice, chased by Hennessy. Using it was undoubtedly one of the worst mistakes of his life. Now, he couldn't stop—willing to do whatever it took to get more. His rent was overdue by over a month, and he knew the landlord would come knocking any day. In just four weeks of using, he had lost almost fifteen pounds, his face hollowing out, a reflection of the shame that kept him hiding from his mother.

He had been avoiding his mother for weeks. She called every other day, her voicemails growing increasingly concerned, urging him to come see her. Nathaniel couldn't bear to face her, not like this. She would know the second she saw him. Her eyes filled with the same disappointment he felt every time he caught a glimpse of his reflection in the mirror. His once-sharp features now looked hollow, his skin pale and gaunt. His body was wasting away, a result of a month-long binge that had stripped him of his formerly healthy appearance. It wasn't just the physical toll—it was the shame. He had become someone she would barely recognize, and the thought of her seeing him like this, broken and addicted, filled him with dread.

Slumped on the edge of his bed, Nathaniel felt the familiar weight of despair pressing down on him. The mattress sagged beneath him, barely supporting his slouched frame. His fingers tightened around the neck of the Hennessy bottle, lifting it to his lips for another slow, deliberate swig. The alcohol burned as it slid down his throat, a harsh reminder of the pain he had come to crave. He had just finished smoking meth, the pungent odor still lingering in the air. The mix of meth and liquor was a dangerous one, a lethal cocktail that promised the high he so desperately sought.

In minutes, it would hit him—hard. The euphoria would wash over him, numbing everything and pushing him deeper into the false comfort of the drug-induced haze. As the warmth of Hennessy spread through his chest, he leaned back against the headboard, closing his eyes and surrendering to the inevitable. The room spun in circles around him, the edges of his vision blurring as reality slipped away. His thoughts became jumbled, muddled by the drugs, sinking him into a dreamlike state where time and consequences no longer mattered. For a moment, there was peace, but he knew the high would fade, the euphoria would slip through his fingers, and then he would do it over and over again.

Nearly eight days later, Nathaniel knew he had avoided his mother for as long as possible. He had to visit her soon, or she would show up at his door—a situation he definitely wanted to avoid. Determined to keep her at bay, he had managed to stay clean for nearly a week. Now, he would go to Sunday dinner, hoping she wouldn't catch on to what he'd been up to.

* * *

"Amen! Hallelujah! Thank you, Father!" Adyleigh Hunter shouted out as she raised her hand in praise.

"I give You total praise!" the combined choir of First Community Baptist Church sang out in harmony.

This particular song always sparked a deep desire in Adyleigh to express her gratitude for all God had done for her. Momentarily forgetting her constant pain, she continued to wave her hand in total praise as tears streamed down her face. When she lowered her hand, it landed in Gabriel's big, waiting hand.

Gabriel, her husband of over twenty years, had never been one to show outward praise. The tapping of his feet to the harmonious sounds from the choir was the best you were going to get. While Adyleigh praised God, Gabriel would watch her reverently. And whenever she raised her hands, his heart ached for her because he knew she was in pain. So, he did what he always did: waited for her to lower her hand so he could massage her fingers.

When Adyleigh felt her husband's warm touch, she turned her head to look at him and mouthed, "Thank you," even as she winced in pain. As she glanced down at her hand in her husband's strong hand, she noticed how much worse her fingers were getting. The skin around them was tight and colorless, and the tips were hardening. No amount of Nivea lotion provided relief, but she was diligent about applying a new layer often. With her fingers in so much pain today, she pondered whether she should have taken her husband up on his offer. On their way to church, Gabriel had suggested they go out to dinner instead of her cooking. She shot him a look that made even him laugh as he backtracked his words.

Their son Nathaniel was coming over for dinner later that evening, and she was excited because he had been canceling their regular family dinners for the past couple of weeks. She couldn't put her finger on it, but as a mother, she sensed something was wrong.

Adyleigh nodded slightly to her husband, reassuring him that she was okay. As Reverend Mitchell gave the final charge for the week, Adyleigh and Gabriel exited the church hand in hand.

* * *

When they got home from morning service, she immediately started preparing Sunday dinner. She was cooking a delightful array of Nathaniel's favorite dishes: smothered chicken, fried catfish, creamy mashed potatoes, collard greens, deviled eggs, and yeast rolls. She also had to make yellow rice because Gabriel didn't like mashed potatoes. For dessert, she had asked Gabriel's sister,

Meeka, to make banana pudding and bake a cake.

Now, sitting on the side of the bed, Adyleigh had just woken up from a much-needed nap. The nap hadn't refreshed her as much as she had hoped. She felt tired, drained, and worried as the images of her dream began to return. She dreamed about her son. Nathaniel needed her, but she couldn't quite make out what was going on.

"Hey, babe, how you feel?" Gabriel asked as he walked into the room carrying a bottle of water in one hand and her afternoon pills in the other.

Her medication included something for pain, acid reflux, high blood pressure, a treatment for skin fibrosis, and the most important pill for pulmonary hypertension.

"Thank you," Adyleigh said as she shared her discomfort about her dream with her husband.

Gabriel eyed Adyleigh, who appeared visibly shaken by the dream. He tried to comfort her by reassuring her that their son would be okay. Gabriel also knew that his wife and son shared an unbreakable bond, so nothing he said would calm her until she laid eyes on him for herself.

While Gabriel was in the other room watching his New York Giants get demolished, Adyleigh was on her knees, offering up prayer.

"Most holy and everlasting Father, I come to you on bended knee and with a humble heart. First, I want to thank you for being so good to me over the years. You have kept me when others said I wasn't going to make it. Father, you have charged me with the care of your son Nathaniel. I pray that you are pleased with my efforts. Father, I come to you asking that you touch your son and help him as he goes through whatever it is he is going through. I ask that you open my eyes so that I may see what is going on with my son. Father, I also ask that you give me more time. Please, Father, grant me more time, for my job here is not done. Amen!"

Once she finished, Adyleigh slowly lifted herself off the floor, now feeling refreshed and energized.

* * *

Sunday dinner had commenced, and Adyleigh sat at the table pushing her food around on the plate. Closely eyeing Nathaniel, she was troubled by his gaunt and disheveled appearance. Each time she stole a glance at him, her heart ached. His fidgety demeanor and the fact that he barely touched his food—especially since Adyleigh had cooked his favorite dishes—further heightened her concern.

"How's work going?" Adyleigh asked, trying to fill the awkward silence with small talk.

"Everything's fine, Mom," Nathaniel replied, avoiding

her eyes.

The lie felt heavy on his tongue, knowing she would see right through it. In truth, he was anything but fine — on probation at work for being late more than five times in the last two weeks. One more slip-up, and he'd be out. For the past week, he had managed to stay clean and arrive on time, but he knew he had to keep it up. He couldn't afford to lose this job.

Adyleigh glanced at her husband, and they exchanged a silent, knowing look, but she decided not to press further.

"How's Shelly? I thought she'd be joining us today," she asked, mentally noting to reach out to Shelly herself, thinking maybe the young woman could shed some light on what was really going on with her son.

"She's good. She told me to tell you hello," Nathaniel replied, this time meeting his mother's gaze.

It was the truth; Shelly had asked about her.

They continued with small talk while Adyleigh quietly observed her son, her concern growing. Sitting at the table, Adyleigh's heart ached at the sight of her son in this condition. She was certain he had been staying away so she wouldn't see how badly he was doing. Looking at her son, she was reminded of the day Dr. Kohn told them she was pregnant.

Nervously shifting in the chair, Adyleigh abandoned the idea of sitting and decided that standing might be a better option. As she walked over to look at the pictures hanging on the wall, she noticed there were new additions to those already displayed. Dr. Kohn was now a grandfather. Apart from that, his office had hardly changed since the last time she was there four years ago.

"Sit down, babe. You're making me nervous with all that moving around," Gabriel pleaded with her.

"I'm sorry, my love. I'm just nervous about what Dr. Kohn is going to say. He's always advised us against having children."

Adyleigh had no doubts in her mind when she was a week late for her menstrual that she was pregnant. She wasn't sure why she chose not to share the news with Gabriel right away. Who was she kidding? She knew exactly why. Her husband would try to persuade her not to have their child. He had always expressed his concern, and he did not make it a secret that if he had to choose between her and their unborn child, he would always choose her. But for Adyleigh, the decision was just as easy. If she had to choose, it would always be her child.

As they waited for Dr. Kohn to join them in his office, she couldn't help but feel anxious. Dr. Kohn hurriedly entered the office, apologizing for keeping them waiting. Adyleigh tried to read his facial expression but couldn't. After the exchange of a few pleasantries, Dr Kohn confirmed what Adyleigh already knew to be true: she was pregnant. He also informed them that the scarring around her lungs had increased. He advised them that with the pregnancy, her lungs could progressively worsen, adding stress to her heart. Due to the type of scleroderma that Adyleigh had, carrying a child to term could be fatal. Furthermore, the medications she had been on for years may have dire consequences for the fetus.

That evening after dinner, Adyleigh and Gabriel prayed that God would help them do what was right for everyone. Adyleigh's prayer was for a healthy baby, even if she had to give her life for him or her. She also dedicated her unborn child to God's care.

Now as she sat watching her son, she prayed once more, reminding God of the promise to take care of her one and only son. She prayed that God did not bless her with her son just for him to struggle like this.

* * *

Nathaniel unlocked the door and stepped into his apartment, the familiar creak of the hinges echoing in the quiet space. He dropped his keys on the counter and let out a deep sigh, running a hand through his hair. Dinner with his parents had been tense, despite the small talk. He knew his mother could sense something was off, but she didn't press him. She never did. The way she looked at him, though, with that mix of concern and quiet fear— it gnawed at him.

Nathaniel's thoughts circled back to her as he collapsed onto the couch. His mother had always been able to read him like a book. She probably thought he was back on drugs. She wouldn't say it aloud, though—she believed in the power of words, believing that speaking something gave it life. Instead, she would pray, taking her worries to God and hoping He would help Nathaniel find his way. He could picture her now, sitting at the edge of her bed, her Bible open, whispering prayers for him. He felt guilty for making her worry. But as bad as things were, at least he had been sober for an entire eight days. For him, that was a record and had to count for something.

His phone buzzed, pulling him from his thoughts. It was Shelly.

I'm on my way, her text read. *I have something to tell you.*

Nathaniel stared at the message, wondering what she could possibly want to tell him now. He hadn't seen her much lately—work had been too chaotic, and their relationship had felt distant for weeks.

It wasn't long before he heard a knock at the door. Shelly stepped inside, her eyes wide and anxious, but there was something else—something almost exciting in her expression. This was a very unfamiliar look, and it had him concerned.

"Nate, I've been meaning to tell you this for a while,"

Shelly began, referring to him by his nickname. "I didn't know how to bring it up, but I can't wait anymore," she continued, her voice trembling a little.

"What's going on?" Nathaniel asked, suddenly afraid of the answer.

A thousand worst-case scenarios flashed through his mind in an instant. But then Shelly took a deep breath and smiled.

"I'm pregnant."

For a moment, the room felt as if it were spinning. Pregnant? He was going to be a father. His mind struggled to catch up and process the weight of her words.

He blinked, his heart racing. "I'm...I'm going to be a dad?"

Shelly nodded, her eyes glistening. "Yes."

A whirlwind of emotions surged through him—fear, joy, disbelief. He couldn't stop the grin spreading across his face despite the shock.

"I'm going to be a dad," he repeated, almost to himself, letting the reality sink in.

He felt a strange sense of peace settle over him, something he hadn't experienced in a long time. For the first time in weeks, perhaps months, there was something to look forward to—something bigger than his struggles, his mistakes.

"I have to tell my parents," he said suddenly, excitement bubbling up inside him.

His mother had always prayed for him to find his way, and now, maybe this was the path he needed. He couldn't wait to see her face when he told her.

But even as the joy flooded in, the weight of responsibility pressed down on him, too. He had to get his life together—not just for himself, but for his child, for Shelly, for the family he was about to build. There was no room for mistakes anymore.

* * *

While washing the last of the dinner dishes, Adyleigh let her tears slowly fall down her face and into the sink where they mingled with the million white suds. When she was done, she felt weighed down, as if the weight of the world had taken residence upon her shoulders. Grabbing the dish towel, Adyleigh dried her hands, noting the blue tint of her fingertips. That couldn't be a good thing.

Weary, Adyleigh dropped her head, feeling a strong desire to pray for her son once more. Just as she whispered "Amen", she felt Gabriel's hands wrap around her, urging her to lie down and get some rest after her full day. Doing a quick glance at the kitchen wall clock, she shrugged off the uneasiness creeping into her spirit as she walked out of the kitchen.

Adyleigh finally gave in to her husband's wishes and decided to go to bed, but not before she prayed. Sitting on the side of the bed, she prayed for Nathaniel, feeling deep down that he was fighting demons that he alone could not handle. As she lay down and closed her eyes, Adyleigh was well aware of the tightening in her chest. All day she had been having difficulty catching her breath. She mustered enough strength to roll over and reach for Gabriel, but then everything went black.

* * *

Adyleigh woke to the constant beeping of machines and the strange, stoic, methodical voices of the doctors who were coming in and out of the hospital room. Adyleigh was able to make out Gabriel's pained, strained voice as he cried and pleaded for her to stay with him. Desperately searching for Nathaniel's voice amid all the noise, she didn't hear him. Instead, she felt the weight of his head resting on her body, willing her not to give up on him. If only he knew that as his mother, Adyleigh would never give up on him. She would lay down her very life for him. Every breath she took was to breathe life into him. In fact, that is exactly what she did when she decided to bring him into the world.

* * *

At sixteen years old, Adyleigh was diagnosed with Scleroderma.

"Schler-a-what?" she remembered asking the doctor.

As Adyleigh sat looking at all the diplomas and degrees hanging on the wall in Dr. Kohn's office, she paid special attention to the family pictures—pictures of his children, family vacations, and various graduation portraits. Adyleigh began to wonder if she would ever be blessed with children and have the opportunity to display their pictures on her office wall one day. The screeching sound of a chair scraping across the polished laminated flooring brought her back to reality.

And just in time to her father's loud, deep baritone voice asking, "What are you talking about sss-derma?" Not quite able to pronounce the word, he abandoned the attempt and said, "I ain't never heard of anything like that. And what do you mean there is no cure?"

Her father kept repeating the words "no cure" while Adyleigh's mother sat silently crying in the chair next to him.

Now looking at the doctor, Adyleigh heard him mention terms like arthritis, rheumatoid arthritis, and lupus. All of this was too much for young Adyleigh to comprehend.

Dr. Kohn turned his body to face Adyleigh directly. He kneeled on one knee and covered Adyleigh's shaking hand with his. Looking into her eyes, he started explaining the disease

Scleroderma. He informed Adyleigh that she had a rare form, and she would need to make some adjustments to her young life. When Adyleigh turned eighteen, it was in the same office that Dr. Kohn had advised her that she shouldn't have children because of the pulmonary arterial hypertension complication from her form of Scleroderma. He explained to her that she could die giving birth if, by some miracle, she carried the child to term.

* * *

Adyleigh was unable to speak or move, but she desperately longed to hold her son in her arms. Silently, she prayed to God for more time; she couldn't leave Nathaniel this way.

Father, how can I possibly rest knowing my child is in so much distress?

Adyleigh lay there unresponsive, but she was still present with them. She continued to plead with God to allow her to help her son. She heard Nathaniel sharing the news that he was going to be a father.

"Mom, I'm going to be a dad. You must come back to us because I need you. I need your guiding hand," he whispered to his mother, praying that it would be the reason she held on.

With that news, Adyleigh turned her head towards

the light. A single tear rolled down her face, and she smiled because she was finally at peace and ready to take her crown. Nathaniel would have a child who would love him unconditionally, and he would not be alone. She trusted God to take care of her son, whom she named Nathaniel because he was a gift from God.

5 Days Later – The Funeral

First Community Baptist Church was filled with the soft hum of voices and the quiet rustling of clothing as mourners settled into the pews. The stained-glass windows cast a kaleidoscope of colors onto the wooden floor, creating a patchwork of light that seemed almost too cheerful for such a somber occasion. The blend of perfumes and colognes from the congregation converged into a sharp, overpowering stench in the air, competing for dominance with the faint fragrance of lilies and roses arranged around the altar.

At the front of the church, a closed casket rested under a cascade of white flowers, their petals pure and delicate against the dark wood. Beside it stood Nathaniel, dressed in an ill-fitting black suit that seemed to reflect the tragedy of the pain he felt within. The suit hung awkwardly on his frame, its baggy shoulders and long sleeves echoing the weight of his grief.

His shoulders were hunched, folding inward as if

trying to shield a heart that was already shattered. His hands trembled as they gripped the edge of the casket. His face was a mask of grief, his eyes red and puffy from crying, yet the tears continued to flow uncontrollably, streaming down his cheeks in a relentless cascade.

Nathaniel's lips quivered, silently mouthing words to his mother that only he and the void between them could hear. He swayed slightly, unsteady on his feet, as if the overwhelming sorrow would knock him down at any moment. Every fiber of his being ached, his body barely holding itself together under the crushing weight of his loss.

The congregation watched with heavy hearts, their shared grief palpable in the room, while Nathaniel stood alone in his pain, each tear a testament to the depth of his love for the mother he had lost.

As the organist began to play one of his mother's favorite songs, "His Eye Is on the Sparrow," Nathaniel felt a fresh wave of sorrow crash over him. The gentle, haunting melody filled the church, each note piercing his heart like a knife. He heard the whispers of the congregation and saw their sympathetic glances, but it all felt distant, like a hazy dream. He couldn't focus on anything except the gaping emptiness that his mother once filled.

His knees buckled slightly, and he gripped the casket

tighter to keep himself upright. The song brought back a flood of memories—Sunday mornings at church, his mother singing this very hymn in her strong, clear voice, her hand clasping his as they swayed to the music. The memory was so vivid that he almost expected to hear her voice rise above the congregation, strong and sure. But there was only silence, save for the soft music and the muffled sobs of those around him. A sob escaped his lips, and he tried to swallow it back down to keep some semblance of composure, but the pain was too much. He felt like a child again, lost and afraid.

Nathaniel dropped to his knees beside the casket, his body shaking from the force of his sobs. The music continued to play, the singer's voice echoing off the high ceilings. Nathaniel was drowning in his grief, unable to breathe, unable to think of anything but the void his mother had left behind. He felt a hand on his shoulder, but he couldn't bring himself to look up. All he could do was cry, his tears falling like rain as his heart broke over and over again.

"Why?" he choked out, his voice barely a whisper. "Why did you have to go?"

The question lingered in the air, unanswered, as the hymn reached its peak. Nathaniel's sobs grew louder, filling the church with a raw, unfiltered pain that brought tears to the eyes of those around him. The hand on his shoulder squeezed gently, offering silent comfort, but it did little to ease the ache in his heart.

As the final notes of the song faded into silence, Nathaniel leaned against the casket, his forehead resting on the cool wood. He closed his eyes, his body racked with shudders. He didn't know how to move forward, how to exist in a world without his mother. All he knew was that the pain was too much to bear, and he felt utterly, irrevocably lost.

30 Days Later...

"God, I can't do this," he muttered to himself, his voice barely a whisper, hoarse and broken. "I can't make it. I just want it to stop."

Nathaniel felt as if he were being ripped apart from the inside out, the withdrawal tearing through him with brutal force. His body was weak, and his spirit felt even weaker. The weight of everything—his mother's death, his own self-destruction—crushed him. He felt as though he were drowning, unable to find his footing, unable to see a way out. But he had to see a way out. He had a baby girl on the way, and failure was not an option.

But then, through the haze of pain and fear, he heard it again—the soft, soothing whisper of his mother's voice. It was just like before, when he lay on the floor, slipping into darkness. Her calm and steady voice filled his mind, cutting through the chaos.

Baby, you've got to get up. You can do this. I'm right here with you, she said, her words filled with a warmth that made him want to cry.

Nathaniel's eyes fluttered open, tears spilling down his cheeks as he clung to the sound of her voice. He knew it wasn't real, knew she wasn't really there, but it didn't matter. It was all he had, the only thing keeping him from giving up entirely.

"Mom?" he croaked, his voice shaky. "I'm scared. I don't know if I can make it."

Yes, you can, Nathaniel, she replied softly. *You're stronger than you think. You've always been strong. I believe in you.*

Her words washed over him, a balm to his aching soul. He wanted to believe her, to find the strength she saw within him. He focused on her voice, letting it guide him and pull him back from the brink.

Every time the pain grew too much, every time he felt like he couldn't take another second, he heard her, felt her presence beside him. She was there, holding his hand, stroking his hair, just like she did when he was a child.

I'm right here, baby, she whispered. *I won't leave you. You're going to get through this. You're going to be okay.*

Nathaniel gripped the sheets, his knuckles turning

white as he fought against the urge to give in. He could feel his mother's love surrounding him, feel her spirit lifting him up and pushing him forward. With each breath, he focused on her voice and the promise that he wasn't alone and could survive this.

And slowly, painfully, he started to believe it. He felt something shifting inside him, a tiny flicker of hope sparking to life in the darkness. It wasn't much, but it was enough to keep him going. Enough to keep him fighting.

"I'm not going to let you down, Mom," he whispered, his voice filled with determination. "I'm going to make it. I promise."

Authors' Bios

Eva Tremaine, a lifelong resident of Queens, is a versatile author whose works include *Secret's Told: A Sister's Betrayal, Open: Love, Lust & Sexuations, Unstable* (a trilogy), *Seven Again: Coming Full Circle*, and *Betrayal Served Cold*. She is also the Founder and CEO of TREMAINE IT Solutions, a software consulting company. A former model, she traded in her runway shoes for a pen to pursue her true love of creating stories that readers will enjoy. Eva now devotes her time to family, reading, writing, traveling, and crafting stories that resonate with readers. Learn more about her at **www.evatremaine.com**.

Alicia J Evans is a resident of Queens and a former NYC Transit Authority Bus Operator for over 25 years. She is a graduate of Queens College, where she received her bachelor's degree in English with a minor in Creative Writing. Her short story "The Bay Window" is an award-winning short story. She has short stories published in LaGuardia Community Colleges online magazine, The Lit, 2021 & 2022 editions. Her debut novel, *I Deserve*, was published in 2022. Her non-fiction book *How I Got Over–My Journey on Overcoming Loss* was published in 2024. Alicia believes there is something magical in weaving words together to tell a tale.

Alicia is the Co-Founder and President of Sugar & Spice Book Club, where she loves to bring authors and readers together for intimate book discussions. She believes reading takes you on a journey, one page at a time. When Alicia is not writing or reading, she can be found entertaining family and friends through her love of hosting. Learn more about her at **www.aliciajevans.com**.

Other Books by Eva Tremaine

Other Books by Alicia J. Evans

I Deserve

How I Got Over — My Journey on Overcoming Loss

Coming Soon: *I Desire*

www.ingramcontent.com/pod-product-compliance
Lightning Source LLC
Chambersburg PA
CBHW051136020726
47501CB00005B/1538